Jerry Scherzinger

THE KIDNAPPER WOUNDED SPRANG STRAIGHT
AT FRANK

*Footprints Under the Window*

THE FEROCIOUS WOLFHOUND SPRANG STRAIGHT
AT FRANK.

*Footprints Under the Window*

# HARDY BOYS MYSTERY STORIES

# FOOTPRINTS UNDER THE WINDOW

By
FRANKLIN W. DIXON

*ILLUSTRATED BY*
J. CLEMENS GRETTA

NEW YORK
GROSSET & DUNLAP
PUBLISHERS

Made in the United States of America

# CONTENTS

iv Contents

# CHAPTER I

### SIDNEY PEBBLES

When Frank and Joe Hardy returned from a hike down the Shore Road one afternoon and found in the mail-box a notice to the effect that a message was awaiting them at the local telegraph office, they were immediately very much excited.

"Hope nothing has happened to Dad and Mother on their trip," exclaimed Frank.

"Maybe it's just a message saying they're coming home," replied Joe. "And I'll be glad, too. Keeping house is all right in its way, but a week of it is plenty."

Frank hastily unlocked the door, strode to the telephone, and called up the telegraph office. He gave his name and asked for the message.

He listened for a moment. Joe, watching,

saw Frank's eyes widen, heard him gasp in dismay.

"What is it? What is it?" asked Joe, nudging him anxiously.

"Goodnight!"

"What is it?" demanded Joe. "Tell a fellow, won't you! What was the message?"

"Aunt Gertrude!"

"Not coming here?"

"Coming here," admitted Frank dolefully.

"Tonight?"

"On the nine-thirty boat."

Joe jerked off his coat and dived toward the sink.

"Now we'll have to clean up the place," he said. "If there is so much as a teacup out of place we'll never hear the end of it. You know Aunt Gertrude."

Yes, they knew Aunt Gertrude. She was an elderly maiden lady whose temper was as uncertain as her age. She had great affection for her two nephews but this affection was carefully concealed. Aunt Gertrude was bossy—in fact, she was a tyrant.

"Seems to me every time the folks go away and we plan to camp out here and have some fun, Aunt Gertrude has to show up," grumbled Frank, as he grabbed a broom.

"That's true," agreed his brother, "but she never kept us from solving any mysteries. Just think how many times when she's been here, we've been on the trail of some crooks."

"Hope she brings a mystery with her this time," laughed Frank.

"Things have been a bit dull lately," Joe reflected, "but they won't be after she gets here!"

Little did he realize at the moment how prophetic his words were.

"She'll think we've been working on a case instead of housekeeping," said Joe, "if she sees this house the way it looks now!"

"Never mind the dishes," said Frank suddenly. "We'll do them later. We'll have to fix up the guest room."

"That's right," agreed Joe, who had been hopping about the kitchen in a frenzy and getting nothing done. "The guest room comes first."

He tore out into the hall and raced upstairs, Frank following. The upper floor of the Hardy home was a scene of violent commotion for the next half hour as the Hardy boys aired rooms, made beds, changed linen and swept floors. Not until the guest room was immaculate did they turn their attention to the linen closet. They were appalled at the quantity of soiled clothing. Both boys had completely forgotten to send their shirts out to the laundry, as well as the other things.

"We'll take them down to Sam Lee," decided Joe. "He's the best Chinese laundryman in town. If we tell him the fix we're in he'll have them all ready by tomorrow."

"Good idea."

They gathered up the linen and stuffed it into the bag. While they were bringing it down stairs the front door opened. Chet Morton, fat, tousle-headed and beaming, stepped into the hall. When Chet spied the laundry bag he chirped:

"Washee? Washee? Any colla's today?"

"Gangway!" shouted Joe. "Rush order for Sam Lee."

"Sam Lee? You can't take that laundry to him," said Chet.

"Why not?"

"He isn't in Bayport any more," Chet informed them. "He sold out to another Chinaman a while back."

"That's tough luck," said Frank. "Aunt Gertrude is springing a surprise visit on us and we have to get this work done in a hurry. We thought we could count on Sam Lee."

"You can't count on the new chap. He isn't like good old Sam," said Chet, shaking his head. "He wouldn't do his own grandmother a favor. Gee, he has a wicked grin."

"Well, I don't care what he looks like," insisted Joe. "If he's in the laundry business

we have a job for him and the sooner he gets
started on it the better for us. Come along,
Chet.''

The boys left the house and hurried down to
the shabby little shop two blocks away. The
name of Sam Lee was still inscribed upon the
signboard that hung above the door, but when
the boys stepped inside they were aware of a
changed atmosphere.

Ordinarily Sam Lee would come hurrying
forward to serve them, quiet, friendly and
smiling. There would be much joking and
high-pitched chatter among Sam Lee's helpers
beyond the partition at the back. But now no
one came. There was no activity whatsoever in
the laundry.

"Maybe it's a holiday," whispered Joe.

Frank was just about to rap on the counter
when he heard a voice. It was that of a Chinaman, deep and diabolical. It sent a chill
through him.

"He nearly die," said the voice slowly.
"Boat velly hot."

"Too young. Him lucky to live," interjected
another voice, sharp and quick.

"No good. Catchee much tlouble sometime.
No likee," returned the first man.

"All right. All right," growled a third man.
He was obviously white, which explained the
fact that his Chinese companions spoke in

pidgin English. "It won't happen again. No use talking——"

There was a sharp exclamation in Chinese, then a silence. A swift pattering of slippers on the floor heralded the approach from beyond the counter of the most villainous-looking Oriental the boys had ever seen. He had a long, lean face with high cheekbones. His head was pointed and almost bald, while a cruel mouth was partly concealed by a drooping wisp of mustache. His eyes were as cold and glittering as those of a snake.

"Why you listen?"

"Where's Sam Lee?" demanded Frank.

"Sam Lee gone. Far away. Back to China. Me Louie Fong. What you want? Why you listen?" snarled the man.

"If that's the way you talk to customers you won't get much business," remarked Joe. "We have some laundry here. We want it done by tomorrow."

"No can do," returned the Chinaman impatiently. He ripped a laundry check from a pad on the counter. "Thlee—fo' day. Not befo'."

"All right," sighed Frank. "Here's the laundry."

Louie Fong seized the soiled linen, tossed Frank the check, and retreated.

"You go 'way now," he snapped. "No listen."

The boys went out into the street.

"Nice man, eh?" grinned Chet.

"I'd hate to meet him in a dark alley," admitted Frank. "He's an ugly-looking one."

They returned to the house. Through Frank's mind was running the fragmentary conversation they had heard in the laundry: "Him nearly die—Him lucky to live—Catchee much tlouble sometime—" There was something sinister about that conversation, something quite as sinister as the atmosphere of the laundry, as sinister as Louie Fong's evil face. He quickly dismissed these thoughts, however, when they entered the house again and plunged into the business of straightening up the premises.

With the help of Chet Morton they had the place in perfect order by nine o'clock that evening. The house had been swept, dusted and aired; the guest room was neat and spotless; even Aunt Gertrude would have difficulty in finding anything to criticize.

"Now," said Frank, "we'll go down to the dock and meet our beloved Aunt."

It was dark when they reached the wharf on Barmet Bay. The boat had not yet pulled in, although they could see the red and green lights

of the vessel far out in the bay. Chet nudged
Frank.

In the shadows beside the passenger office
on the dock they saw three dark figures. They
were small, neatly-dressed Orientals talking
earnestly together. One of the men seemed
excited, and raised his voice. Though the boys
could not hear what he said they recognized
the tones. It was the sharp, quick voice of one
of the men who had been talking with Louie
Fong that afternoon.

One of his companions laid a hand on his
arm, gesturing toward the boys nearby. The
man glanced back, mumbled something, and
then the trio moved off into the shadows.

"If Louie Fong were there he'd probably
come over and accuse us of spying on them,"
laughed Chet.

In a few moments the boat's whistle sounded
and slowly the big vessel came to rest at the
dock. The boys waited patiently by the gangplank while passengers disembarked, but there
was no sign of Aunt Gertrude.

"That's odd," muttered Frank. "Usually
she's right at the head of the parade. Aunt
Gertrude won't take second place to anyone."

"Maybe she missed the boat," Chet suggested.

"After all the work we did!" groaned Joe.

It was soon evident that Aunt Gertrude had

not taken passage. The lads were at a loss
to account for it, as punctuality was one of
that lady's most prominent virtues.

At that moment there came racing down the
gangplank a young man, good-looking, pleasant-faced, and neatly dressed. He glanced in-
quiringly at the three boys.

"I must telephone right away," he announced, "and I don't want to miss the boat.
Is there a booth here?"

"There's one in the waiting room," replied Joe.

"We'll show you," volunteered Frank, es-
corting the stranger inside. "And we'll let
you know when the boat's warning whistle
blows."

"Thank you," said the young man, striding
across the room.

To the amazement of the boys they saw a
Chinaman, who had been sitting on one of the
benches, get up quickly and go over toward the
newcomer. At once the two entered into an
earnest conversation.

"It seems we're bound to bump into Chinamen at every turn today," laughed Frank.

"You're right," agreed Joe. "Well, that
young man had better hurry up with his phone
call, or he'll miss the boat."

The stranger evidently realized this, for he
stepped into the booth and closed the door

tightly. Joe and Chet sauntered out to the dock, but Frank walked slowly toward the back of the waiting room.

He could hear the traveller from the boat shouting into the mouthpiece, but paid no heed. Suddenly his attention was arrested by the number being given to the operator—it was the telephone number of the Hardy home.

Just as Frank was about to go over to ask the young man what his message was, there came a sudden blast of the steamer's whistle. Joe and Chet rushed into the waiting room.

"Tell the man the boat's ready to leave!"

At the same moment the stranger in the booth began to shout frantically and bang on the door, as he struggled to get out.

"He's locked in!" exclaimed Joe.

"Let me out! Let me out!" shouted the prisoner. "I must catch that boat."

The boys wrenched and tugged at the door, but it would not open. They heard the last blast of the whistle, and the clamor of the engines together with the shouts of the deckhands as the vessel began to pull away from the dock. The exasperated fellow hurled himself at the obstinate door, spluttering with anger.

The joint efforts of the group, however, met with failure. Frank ran out, leaving the others still struggling with the door, and found

Constable Riley of the Bayport police force standing on the wharf watching the receding boat as it steamed off into the bay.

"Mr. Riley, Mr. Riley," he said. "There's a man locked in the telephone booth."

Constable Riley stared at him.

"Huh?" he said.

"There's a man locked in the telephone booth."

"What telephone booth?" asked Riley densely.

"In the waiting room. He can't get out."

"Why did he lock himself in?" asked Riley.

"He didn't. The door jammed. He's missed his boat."

"That was a foolish thing to do," said Riley gravely. "And you want me to help open the door?" This fact having dawned on him he took a small book out of his pocket and laboriously thumbed the pages. "Bein' a constable of the city police force," he said thoughtfully, "I don't know whether I'm within my rights by interferin' with the property of a private corporation. The telephone company owns the booth and the boat company owns the waitin' room, so if I don't get into trouble with one I'm likely to get into trouble with the other. I don't think I've got authority——"

"Oh, forget your old authority," exclaimed Frank. "You won't get into trouble with anyone. The man is locked in. You don't want him to stay there all night, do you?"

"I'd have to arrest him for trespassing if he did," mumbled Riley, inspecting the book. "Nobody is allowed to stay in the waitin' room all night, much less in the telephone place. I guess mebbe I'd better get him out of there."

The officer nearly wrecked the booth in his efforts to release the prisoner, but the door was finally opened and the young man emerged, red-faced and angry.

"What a nuisance!" he expostulated. "I've missed my boat just because of that confounded door."

"How did it happen?" asked Joe curiously.

"I don't know. When I went to open it I found it was jammed, that's all."

"Pardon me," interrupted Frank, "but I overheard you giving the telephone number of our house."

"Oh, are you the Hardy boys?"

"I'm Frank Hardy. This is my brother Joe. And this is Chet Morton."

"I'm glad to know you," said the traveller, putting out his hand to shake. "My name is Sidney Pebbles."

"What message were you trying to telephone to us?" asked Frank.

"I'm afraid it isn't very good news," replied Sidney Pebbles.

# CHAPTER II

## THE MYSTERIOUS GUEST

THE Hardy boys waited tensely to hear the bad news that Sidney Pebbles was about to give them.

"Has—has something happened to our father and mother?" asked Frank.

"No—no," replied the young man. "It's about your aunt."

"Has anything happened to her?" asked Joe.

"Well—nothing fatal," said Sidney Pebbles, "but serious enough to prevent her from taking the boat."

"Was she badly hurt?" asked Frank.

Although Aunt Gertrude did make the boys toe the mark, nevertheless they had a genuine affection for the good lady.

"She injured herself, tripping over a loose plank in the dock just before the boat left. Gave her ankle a bad wrench. She asked me to telephone you at Bayport and tell you she'd come along as soon as she was able."

"It's too bad," commented Joe. "Maybe we ought to try to get in touch with her."

13

"Oh, it isn't serious enough to get worried about, I'm sure," said Pebbles. "Your aunt was more shaken up than anything else. She should be all right in a day or so."

"I'm sorry to hear about your relative," said Chet, "but I'm sorry, too, for the steamship company."

"How's that?" asked Joe.

"She's apt to sue them from here to the Supreme Court," snickered Chet.

At this moment Constable Riley fished out his notebook.

"I'll have to make out a report about this smashed telephone booth," he announced. "Now, young feller, your name and address, please. Your age and profession, color of your eyes, height, weight——"

"Report!" snorted Pebbles indignantly. "I don't have to get my name in the police records just because I couldn't open the door of a telephone booth, do I? When can I catch the next boat, that's what I want to know."

"The next boat south doesn't leave until ten o'clock tomorrow morning," Chet informed him. "You'll have to spend the night in Bayport."

Sidney Pebbles looked dismayed.

"All my luggage is on the boat," he said.

Frank and Joe looked at each other. They were sorry for the young man in his predicament—a predicament caused entirely on their account.

"Why not come and spend the night with us?" Frank suggested. "We're alone at the house and we have a spare room. You're welcome if you'd like to do that."

"Why, that's very good of you," returned Pebbles gratefully. "If you're sure I'm not putting you to any trouble——"

"It ain't regular," muttered Constable Riley as he put his notebook away. "By rights I ought to make a complete report about this affair. Who's going to pay for the damage to that telephone booth?"

"The company," said Sidney Pebbles promptly. "Their doors shouldn't jam."

As it happened, however, it had not been the fault of the telephone company that the door had jammed.

Leaving the dock, the boys brought Sidney Pebbles to their house. Frank was puzzled by the incident of the telephone booth. He was convinced that the door could not have become stuck accidentally, and he wondered if the Chinaman to whom Sidney Pebbles had been talking could have had anything to do with the affair.

"Better stay for a while," Joe said to Chet. "You don't have to go home just yet. We'll make some lemonade, and get a bite to eat."

It was a warm night, and while Frank went to the kitchen, Chet and Joe opened the windows which had been closed during the boys' absence from the house. Sidney Pebbles took off his coat and hung it over the back of a chair. The inside of the garment was plainly visible, and from the inner pocket projected the end of a legal-looking document with heavy red seals.

"Are you on a vacation?" asked Joe.

Sidney Pebbles shook his head.

"No," he said briefly. "Just a business trip. It's annoying to miss that boat because I lose an entire day, but I suppose I'll just have to wait until tomorrow."

"Are you a traveller?" asked Chet.

"No, I'm not a traveller," returned Pebbles. But he volunteered nothing more. He did not even tell them where he came from. It was obvious that he was a very close-mouthed young man so the boys did not press their inquiries further.

They all enjoyed the refreshments which Frank brought in. During the course of the evening Joe laughingly mentioned the work they had done in straightening up the house before Aunt Gertrude's arrival and told of their experience with the new Chinaman, Louie Fong.

"It's strange," he said, "how Sam Lee moved out of Bayport without saying goodbye to anyone."

"That story reminds me of an incident in my own home town," said Pebbles. "We had a laundryman named Joe Sing who was very popular. One morning he disappeared and there was a new Chinaman in the laundry. He didn't know anything about Joe Sing, he said. About a week later I was returning home late at night and I met Joe Sing on the street.

" 'When did you come back, Joe?' " I asked the Chinaman.

"He shook his head and said: 'Me not Joe. Me Charlie Wu.'

"Well, I was positive he was Joe Sing but I didn't argue the matter. Two days later I went into the laundry and there was Joe Sing behind the counter, as large as life. I asked him if he hadn't met me on the street but he said he had just returned from New York that morning. Next day I passed the place and found the laundry closed. Both Joe Sing and the other Chinaman had disappeared and no one in town ever saw them again."

"What do you think was behind it all?" said Joe.

Pebbles shrugged. "Who knows?"

He took his watch chain from his pocket and on the end of it the boys saw a peculiar charm. It was triangular in shape, made of a transparent green substance in the centre of which was a tiny silver serpent.

"Joe Sing gave me that charm one Christmas," said Pebbles, handing the little object around the group. "Odd thing, isn't it?"

Chet looked up suddenly.

"Rain!"

They listened. The unmistakable drumming of rain on the roof could be plainly heard. Chet grabbed his hat.

"I'll get a ducking if I don't race for home," he said.

"I'm afraid you'll get a ducking anyway," said Frank.

"The rain is just starting. I'll go so fast in that car of mine, I'll dodge between the drops."

"Goodnight," he shouted, as he streaked through the hall. "See you in the morning." He was over the threshold like a bullet, had slammed the door, and in another moment those in the house heard the clamorous uproar of the roadster.

"I guess we might as well go to bed," said Pebbles. "It's mighty kind of you fellows to put me up for the night."

"No trouble at all," they assured him. "It was good of you to tell us about Aunt Gertrude. If you hadn't got off the boat to give us that message you wouldn't have been left behind."

The young man picked up his coat. Frank

noticed that he folded it carefully to hide the document with the red seals. They showed him upstairs to the guest room, saw that he was comfortable for the night, then went to their own room.

The rain had settled to a steady downpour.

"I think I'll dream of Chinamen tonight," yawned Frank as he took off his shoes. "What with Sam Lee and Louie Fong and the Chinamen on the dock——"

"And the Chinaman who talked to Mr. Pebbles, and that story he told us," added Joe.

However, neither of the lads dreamed of Chinamen, for they slept heavily. Even the storm that raged the greater part of the night did not arouse them. When they awakened in the morning their first thoughts were for their visitor.

Frank slipped into his dressing-gown and went across the hall. He knocked at the door of the guest room. There was no answer. He knocked again.

While Frank is waiting for an answer to his summons, we may take advantage of the moment to introduce the Hardy boys more clearly to those readers who have not already made their acquaintance in previous volumes of this series.

Frank and Joe Hardy were the sons of Fenton Hardy, a detective who won fame with the

New York Police Department and who retired
to conduct a private detective business of his
own. He had moved to Bayport, a pleasant
city of fifty thousand people on Barmet Bay,
and there his fame as one of the greatest of
American detectives had grown. Great business firms, private individuals and even the
government had entrusted him with many delicate and difficult cases.

Although his sons, Frank and Joe, were still
in High School they had already determined
upon their choice of profession. Each meant
to be a detective like his father. Opportunities
to prove their worth had fallen their way and
they had solved a number of mysteries that had
baffled the Bayport police and—on one occa-
sion at least—their father as well. With luck
and ingenuity they had won such local reputa-
tions as amateur sleuths of more than ordinary
ability that they had obtained their father's
consent to follow in his footsteps.

In the first volume of this series, "The Hardy
Boys: The Tower Treasure," has been related
the story of the first mystery successfully
solved by the boys, a story based on the con-
fession of a dying criminal. Their success had
led to many other cases, and in the immediately
preceding volume of the series, "While the
Clock Ticked," the lads aided in vindicating
a man accused of crime, and had many stirring

adventures in a spooky house with a secre room.

Now, as Frank waited outside the closed door, he was on the threshold of one of the most puzzling and sensational mysteries that had ever confronted the Hardy boys.

"What's the matter?" asked Joe, joining him in the hall. "Can't you waken him?"

Frank knocked loudly. Then he opened the door. The boys looked inside.

"Why, he's gone!" exclaimed Frank.

The room was deserted. The bed had been slept in but Sidney Pebbles had disappeared.

A tiny object lying on the floor was the only reminder of their recent guest. Joe picked it up, and found it to be the little green watch charm. The boys looked at each other, completely bewildered.

"Can you beat that?" said Joe at last. "He cleared out during the night, without even saying goodbye. Ungrateful, I'll say."

"Perhaps he's downstairs," Frank suggested.

At that moment, from the lower floor of the house, they heard a heavy thud. It was followed by a scream—the high, shrill scream of a woman!

# CHAPTER III

## AUNT GERTRUDE

"WHAT was that?" gasped Joe.

Without a word Frank wheeled and raced toward the head of the stairs, Joe close upon his heels. As they ran down toward the lower hall they could hear groans.

Frank reached the living room first. There he stopped short with an exclamation of amazement.

"Aunt Gertrude!"

On the floor beside the couch, lay their aunt. She was moaning and rubbing her head, apparently half-stunned and too weak to get up.

"Aunty!" shouted Joe. "How did you get here?"

Their relative opened her eyes and looked at them.

"Help me up," she muttered. "I don't feel well."

They were at her side in a moment and helping her to her feet. Aunt Gertrude shook her head in a dazed manner, then sat down heavily on the sofa.

"I fell off the couch," she said.

"But how did you get here?" they asked. "How did you reach Bayport when you missed the boat?"

Aunt Gertrude glared at them with some of her old-time fire.

"Nonsense!" she snapped. "I didn't miss the boat."

"But we met the boat last night. Mr. Pebbles said you hurt your ankle."

"Mr. Pebbles?" said Aunt Gertrude thickly. "Who is Mr. Pebbles?"

"Don't you remember? You told him to tell us you had hurt your ankle," said Frank.

"I didn't tell anyone any such thing," retorted the irate lady. She rubbed her forehead. "Such a headache!" she exclaimed. "I didn't hurt my ankle. You must be dreaming."

The boys were puzzled. They realized that Aunt Gertrude was not herself but they could not account for her presence in the house unless the story told by Sidney Pebbles had been fictitious.

"How did you come here?" asked Frank.

"On the boat. On the boat, of course," she said. "I came here at some unearthly hour in the middle of the night. The door was open so I came right in. What else would I do? I didn't want to disturb anyone so I decided to rest on the couch here. I was feeling mighty

sleepy, anyway. I'm sleepy now. I don't know
what's the matter with me. Everything seems
to be going around and around.''

"I don't think you're well, Aunt Gertrude,"
said Joe in concern.

"Of course I'm not well," she snapped.
"I'm feeling very ill. I've been ill ever since
I woke up and found myself on the boat last
night."

"Then you *were* on the boat?"

"Of course I was on the boat!" stormed
their aunt. "Don't ask so many silly questions. I've told you a hundred times that I
was on the boat. I sent you a telegram that
I would be on the boat. Was it my fault if I
fell asleep and got carried past Bayport?"

That, then, was the explanation. Aunt Gertrude had fallen asleep and had been carried
past her destination. She had remained on
the boat until it reached Bayport on the return
voyage, had come at once to the Hardy home
and had gone to sleep on the couch. There was
something very strange about the whole business, however. It was not at all like Aunt Gertrude to be content with sleeping on the couch,
regardless of what hour she arrived. And it
was quite plain that this was not the old, vigor-
ous, stormy, scolding Aunt Gertrude of other
visits. Her face was white, and she seemed
tired and ill.

"I can't figure out why this chap Pebbles should tell us that story about you," said Frank. "It was all a lie from beginning to end. He said you tripped over a loose plank on the dock and hurt your ankle so you couldn't go on the boat."

"I don't know anything about any Mr. Pebbles," insisted Aunt Gertrude. "Nor any loose plank nor—nor anything. I don't feel well. There was a young man on the boat, I remember."

"Good-looking fellow in a gray suit?" asked Joe quickly.

"Yes. He wore a gray suit. He was very nice. I told him I was coming to visit my nephews. He got me a drink of water once."

"Did you talk to any other strangers?" asked Frank.

Aunt Gertrude admitted that she had. Everybody, she insisted, had been very kind to her on the boat.

"Don't ask me any more about it," she ordered. "I'm too dizzy. I don't feel well. I think I'd better go to bed. I had a terrible dream about a Chinaman. Or was it a dream? There isn't a Chinaman in the house, is there?"

"No. Of course not," said Frank.

"Then it must have been a dream. I thought I saw a Chinaman come sneaking in through the window." Aunt Gertrude shuddered. "Ah, he was an ugly brute. But it must have been a dream.''

"This beats anything I ever heard of," Joe muttered. "Pebbles comes here and clears out without a word to anyone and now we find Aunt Gertrude in the house."

Their relative got to her feet.

"I'm going to bed," she muttered.

"Would you like some hot coffee, Aunt Gertrude?" asked Frank.

"I think it would do me good. Bring it upstairs to me. And bring up my suitcase, too, like a good lad."

She swayed and would have fallen had not Joe grasped her by the arm. The boys were greatly disturbed by their aunt's plight. They helped her to the second floor and put the guest room in order. Then they went down to the kitchen and made some coffee.

"Don't you think we'd better call a doctor?" suggested Frank.

"We'll wait a while. Maybe she'll feel better after she's had some breakfast."

The strange disappearance of Sidney Pebbles bothered them. They could not understand why the young man should steal away as he had done.

"Do you think he was a robber?" asked Joe suddenly.

"A robber? He didn't steal anything."

"How do we know?" demanded Joe in excitement. "We haven't looked around. That story about Aunt Gertrude may have been a ruse to get into the house. Maybe he locked himself in the telephone booth in the hope that we would ask him to stay here over night."

The boys hurriedly made a round of the lower part of the house. They inspected the silver, they investigated the cash-box in their father's office where the household spending money was kept, yet nothing seemed to be missing. When the coffee was ready and they had brought it up to Aunt Gertrude, they took advantage of the opportunity to make a thorough search of the guest room in which Sidney Pebbles had slept.

"There are some of Dad's suits in the closet," Frank remembered. "He might have stolen them."

They opened the closet door and looked inside. Ordinarily there were three or four of Mr. Hardy's business suits hanging neatly upon their hangers. Now one of them lay in a huddle upon the floor, and the others had been disturbed. A blue coat had been replaced with a gray pair of trousers. As the boys had paid special attention to the closet the previous evening when they had been setting the room in order, they were positive that no one but Sidney Pebbles had disturbed the garments.

"So!" exclaimed Joe. "That's what he was after. But why didn't he steal the suits?"

"He wasn't after the suits," returned Frank as he turned one of the coats inside out. "Look! Those papers are gone!"

It seemed now that they had arrived at the explanation of the sudden and mysterious departure of their guest.

# CHAPTER IV

## THE FOOTPRINTS

HASTILY the Hardy boys examined each of the suits in the closet. They had noticed, on the previous evening, that the inside pocket of every coat had contained papers and letters. Now every pocket was empty.

"Do you know if any of the papers were important?" asked Joe.

Frank shook his head.

"I haven't the slightest idea. They looked like business letters. There might have been important papers among them."

"What's the matter?" asked Aunt Gertrude faintly.

"That fellow Pebbles went through the pockets of Dad's suits," explained Frank. "He took all the papers from them."

Aunt Gertrude sipped her coffee.

"Tell the police!" she said.

This suggestion, however, did not meet with the favor of the Hardy boys. When they encountered a mystery they were accustomed to making it their own. In this case, moreover, there was good reason why the police should not be called. They knew that Mr. Hardy had been working on an important case, so secret and confidential that he had never hinted at its details. It was more than possible that the missing papers might be concerned with this case. If the police were called in, the nature of the documents might become known and much of Fenton Hardy's careful work would thereby be undone.

Aunt Gertrude groaned and thrust the coffee cup aside.

"I can't drink this coffee," she said. "I don't want any breakfast."

"Don't want any breakfast!" gasped Joe. This was a sure sign that Aunt Gertrude wasn't well. She could ordinarily eat a morning meal that would suffice for two women of her size.

"No, I'm not well. Go away and leave me," she commanded pettishly. "I want to go to sleep."

Obediently the boys tiptoed out of the room. When they went downstairs Frank stepped over to the telephone.

"I'm going to tell Chet about this business," he said. "He'll never forgive us if we leave him out of it."

"He may be able to suggest something, too," replied Joe.

However, when Frank telephoned their chum

he found that the plump boy was already excited over news of his own.

"I was just going to call you," he said when he heard Frank's voice on the wire. "Did you hear about the fight last night?"

"No. What happened?"

"Oh, there was a whale of a battle down on the docks," said Chet. "Regular riot. Half a dozen Chinese were mixed up in it. One of them was stabbed and had to be taken to a hospital. Another was heaved into the water and nearly drowned."

It flashed into Frank's mind that Chinamen seemed to enter this strange affair at every turn. There was the disappearance of Sam Lee, the strange conversation in the laundry, the Chinamen on the dock, the strange Chinaman who had spoken to Sidney Pebbles in the waiting room, the Chinese charm in the guest room, the evil Chinaman of Aunt Gertrude's dream. And now, this sensational battle among Chinamen on the docks.

"Was Louie Fong mixed up in the fight?"

"I don't know. I didn't hear any names. It's strange, though, that since that fellow blew into town we seem to be running into Chinamen at every turn."

"We have a little mystery of our own," said Frank.

"Mystery?" exclaimed Chet eagerly.

"You remember our guest last night?"

"Pebbles? Sure. What's happened?"

"He cleared out during the night after going through the pockets of all Dad's business suits."

Chet's whistle of amazement sounded clearly over the telephone.

"So that's the sort of lad he was! Did he take anything else?"

"Nothing, so far as we know. He left his Chinese charm behind him, by the way. But there is more to it than that. The story he told us about Aunt Gertrude was all a lie."

"What was the idea?" squeaked Chet.

"That's what we can't figure out. Aunt Gertrude was in the house when we woke up this morning. She fell asleep on the boat. I think she was doped. She has been feeling queer ever since we found her lying on the floor——"

"On the floor!"

"Sure. She fell asleep on the couch and tumbled out. She's been acting strangely—says she dreamed there was a Chinaman in the house last night——"

"Say!" exclaimed Chet. "I'm coming over to see you. I have a feeling that you are going to need me."

The receiver clicked. Chet would be on his way to the Hardy home as fast as the old roadster could carry him.

The boys had breakfast, and although they talked over the strange affair from every angle they could arrive at no satisfactory conclusion. Joe was of the opinion that they should start out at once in search of Sidney Pebbles, but Frank shook his head.

"We can't leave Aunt Gertrude, in the first place," he said. "If she isn't feeling a great deal better in the next hour or so I'm going to send for the doctor. As for Pebbles, he won't go near the docks because he knows we'll go there first. We could send Chet down about boat time to look for him but I don't think the man will show up."

"I'm worried about Aunt Gertrude myself," Joe admitted. "I'm sure she must have been doped."

"But why?"

"That's the mystery. If Pebbles merely wanted to get into the house and steal the papers he didn't have to work out such a wild scheme as that."

"I'm going to take a look around the place," said Frank, finishing his meal. "We haven't really made any search for clues."

They left the breakfast table and carefully inspected all the rooms in the lower part of the house. They found a small, muddy mark in the front hall but they agreed that it might have been left by Aunt Gertrude when she entered the house early that morning. On the sill of the living room window they found a number of tiny scratches.

"I don't remember having seen those marks before," said Joe thoughtfully.

"Neither do I. Do you think Pebbles went out through the window?"

"Why should he? The front door wasn't locked."

Frank looked out the window.

"That's interesting," he muttered.

"What do you see?"

"Look there, in the mud."

Beneath the window, in the soil left wet after the night's rain, they saw a footprint clearly outlined. It was quite distinct in the moist clay.

Frank hastened toward the back door.

"This will bear looking into," he said in evident excitement.

Joe followed, and the brothers ran outside, turning toward the side of the house. There, beneath the window, they found not one footprint but half a dozen, all leading toward the path that met the front walk.

"Footprints under the window!" exclaimed Frank Hardy wonderingly. "What do they mean?"

# CHAPTER V

## THE DOCTOR'S ORDERS

The Hardy boys were careful to stay well away from the footprints for fear of destroying them, but from where they stood they were able to read a fragmentary story from those tell-tale marks in the wet clay.

"Someone," said Frank, "came from the grass toward the window. He came very close to the window. Then the footprints show that he went away toward the front path. To get to the path he must have walked across the grass."

"Why did he go to the window?"

"Either to look inside or to climb inside."

The boys examined the part of the house beneath the window. The sill was not far from the ground and they could not determine whether or not anyone had gained entrance to their home in that manner, for there were no marks on the woodwork.

"Maybe the footprints were made by Sidney Pebbles," Joe suggested.

"We should measure them, anyway."

Joe went into the house and returned with a measuring tape, a pencil and a sheet of paper. The boys selected one of the footprints and made careful measurements. Then, on the paper, they inscribed a rough diagram of the sample print.

"Looks like a size six shoe," said Frank in surprise. "That's quite small. Why, mine is an eight."

"That means, then," observed Joe, "that the footprints couldn't have been made by Pebbles. He was about a head taller than either of us. I don't think he has a particularly small foot."

"And yet, who else could have left those footprints? They were made after the rain stopped."

"How do you know?"

"If they had been made before the downpour, they'd have been washed away."

While they were considering this they heard the siren of an automobile and the familiar clatter of Chet Morton's roadster. It drew up at the curb, jolted to a stop, and their fat chum vaulted over the side without the formality of opening the door. He ran across the lawn toward them.

"What's new?" he demanded. "You haven't found Pebbles lying in his gore, have you?"

Frank gestured toward the footprints.

"Those are our only clues," he said.

"Footprints, eh?" exclaimed Chet. "Good work. Feetmarks are my dish. Hmm!" He surveyed them gravely. "Well, they tell a plain story. Somebody jumped out of the upstairs window, started off toward the front walk, changed his mind and went back toward the garage. Have you looked to see if your motorcycles are stolen?"

"If he jumped out of an upstairs window," said Frank, "he must have been a butterfly. He would have sunk into mud to his ankles. And as for going to the garage, he must have walked backwards if he did."

Chet was crestfallen.

"Maybe I'm wrong," he admitted. "However, I'll bet he took a motorcycle."

Investigation of the garage, however, revealed the motorcycles and the Hardy boys' roadster safe and unharmed.

"As a detective, Chet," grinned Joe, "you'd better go and take a seat near the back of the hall."

"Well, I don't know all the facts in the case," said the fat one, quite undisturbed. "Tell me what happened."

They related the full story of the events of the morning. When Chet was told of Aunt Gertrude's dream he became vastly excited.

"There you are!" he said grandly. "There's your whole mystery in a nutshell."

"What do you mean?" asked Joe.

"It wasn't a dream. She did see a real Chinaman. He crawled through the living room window, and went upstairs to steal the papers from your father's coats. He didn't expect to find anyone in the guest room. Pebbles was there. Pebbles tackled the robber. The Chinaman throttled Pebbles, carried the body downstairs, took the corpse away and threw it into the bay. It's simple. Boy, what a ghastly crime!"

Chet was quite serious as he outlined this horrible explanation of the night's doings.

"Do you mean to say a Chinaman could murder someone in the room next to us and we wouldn't hear a sound?" chided Frank incredulously.

"I know how you fellows sleep," Chet assured them. "A Fourth of July celebration could be held in the next room and you wouldn't wake up."

"Your theory is full of holes," said Joe.

"You don't like that theory?" asked Chet cheerfully. "All right, then. Here's another. We strive to please. Pebbles got into the house to steal the papers. He took them and knew he would be suspected——"

"Naturally."

"He knew he would be suspected so he went around to the side of the house and left footprints under the window. Why should he leave footprints under the window when he could get out by the front door, which wasn't locked? So you would think the footprints were made by someone who didn't know the door was open. Then, when he saw Aunt Gertrude asleep in the living room he disguised himself as a Chinaman and walked back and forth until she woke up and saw him.''

"That theory," scoffed Frank, "is even crazier than the first."

"Oh, well," sighed Chet, "if you don't *want* my help, go ahead and solve the mystery by yourselves.''

At that moment the boys heard a cry from within the house.

"Aunt Gertrude!" said Frank. "She's calling us."

Quickly they ran upstairs. The moment they entered the guest room they saw that their relative was really ill. Her face was flushed with fever and she tossed restlessly on the bed.

"I—I think you'd better get the doctor, Frank," she said feebly. "I don't feel well at all.''

Frank hurried downstairs to the telephone. He called the office of the family physician, Dr. Bates, and explained the circumstances.

"I'll be right up," said the doctor.

While they were awaiting his arrival they

did what they could to make their aunt more comfortable, but it was evident that her condition was growing worse. Her mind seemed to be wandering and she spoke frequently of the Chinaman she had seen in her dream.

"Such an evil face!" she repeated again and again.

"I don't believe it was a dream at all," Chet insisted. "There was a real, live Chinaman in this house last night."

"I don't know what to make of the whole strange business," Frank confessed.

When the doctor arrived a few minutes later the boys told him how Aunt Gertrude had fallen asleep on the boat, how she had entered the house in the early hours of the morning, and how they had discovered her in the living room.

"Certainly something must have happened," he agreed. "She was in good health when she left her home?"

"I don't think she would have started for Bayport if she hadn't been feeling well," said Frank.

The boys had said nothing about Sidney Pebbles and the affair of the missing papers.

The doctor went upstairs. He was with Aunt Gertrude for a short time and when he returned his face was grave.

"Would anyone have a motive for doping your aunt?" he asked.

"That's what has been puzzling us," said Joe. "We thought she might have been doped but we can't imagine why. She said she spoke to several strangers on the boat and that one man got her a drink of water."

"There is no doubt," said the doctor, "that she is suffering from the effects of some kind of drug. She is feeling the after-effects now. As a matter of fact, she is quite ill and she is likely to become worse. Her system couldn't stand the strain. Where are your parents?"

"They're away on a trip," Frank told him.

"Well, I'd advise you to get a nurse to look after her. I know a woman who will be glad to come here for a few days until your aunt is on her feet again. Do you want me to send her here?"

"If you think best, Doctor," said Frank.

"I do think it best," he replied seriously. The physician took out his pen and notebook and scribbled on a pad. "You can get this prescription filled at the corner drug store and it will help your aunt's condition. I'll send the nurse around right away and I'll drop in myself this evening."

"Thank you, Doctor," they said.

He left the prescription and picked up his hat.

"Can't understand it," muttered Dr. Bates. "Why anyone should go to the trouble of doping a harmless lady—it's beyond me."

"Aunt Gertrude hasn't an enemy in the world," remarked Joe.

"Well, if I were you I should try to get in touch with Mr. and Mrs. Hardy right away and ask them to come home."

"We'll do our best," they promised.

The doctor went away. Chet was nearly pop-eyed with excitement.

"Doped!" he exclaimed. "That explains the whole business. It's as clear as mud."

"What's your theory now?" asked Frank.

Chet was solemn as he explained his newest brain-wave.

"Kidnapers!" he said. "They doped your aunt and planned to hold her for ransom."

"Why didn't they, then?" said Joe.

Chet was nonplussed.

"That," he said, "is the mystery."

"You're a lot of help," observed Frank. "If anyone drugged Aunt Gertrude with the idea of kidnaping her, then why on earth didn't they hold her? As soon as that nurse arrives I think we'll see if we can't dig up a few theories of our own."

"Why do you need more theories?" demanded Chet with great indignation. "I've given you three or four of them. All good ones, too. I tell you, I'm not appreciated here. I spend a lot of hard work on this case and all I get is the horse-laugh. What have you in the way of food? It's almost an hour since I had breakfast."

He ambled off into the kitchen, quite undisturbed by the reception his precious theories had received, and reappeared in a moment with a tremendous wedge of pie.

"I always think better when I'm eating," he explained. "I'll have some more smart ideas for you in a few minutes."

Frank got up from his chair.

"Come on," he said. "Let's go back and look at those footprints again."

# CHAPTER VI

## CHINESE WRITING

It was fortunate that Chet Morton was a good-natured youth, otherwise he might have gone away in a huff because his brilliant suggestions had been so casually dismissed by the Hardy boys. However, nothing ever disturbed Chet and a piece of pie was always enough to soothe his feelings. Quite as if he had never ventured a suggestion at all, he left the house with the Hardy boys and they again examined the mysterious footprints under the window.

The slice of pie was so large and Chet was so busy demolishing it, that he expressed no more theories. The boys examined the lawn carefully to see if they could find any more footprints but in this they were unsuccessful for there were no marks in the springy turf.

"We'll have a hard time finding this fellow Pebbles," Joe declared. "As a matter of fact, I don't think Pebbles was his name at all."

"If he meant to steal Dad's papers it isn't likely that he would give us his right name," agreed Frank.

"He was using an anonymous, eh?" mumbled Chet, with his mouth full of pie.

"A what?"

"An anonymous. I mean," amended Chet hastily, "he was using a *nom de plume*."

"You mean an alias," said Frank.

"In plain English," said Chet, "I mean he wasn't using his right name."

"That's what I said in the first place," declared Joe.

Chet nodded.

"I quite agree with you." He ventured toward a clump of bushes along the side of the house, idly kicking aside the branches with his toe.

Suddenly he stuffed the last of the pie-crust into his mouth, uttered a gurgle of triumph and dived into the bushes.

"What now?" said Joe.

"Got it! Got it!" mumbled Chet, emerging from the bushes with something clutched in his hand. "I told you I might find something. It's a clue. And I'll bet it has your old footprints beaten all hollow."

The Hardy boys came over, curious to know what Chet had discovered. He opened his hand carefully, as if he had captured a butterfly and was afraid it would escape from his grasp.

"What is it?" asked Frank.

In Chet's hand they saw a folded fragment of paper. At first the boys were inclined to make light of the find as being an ordinary scrap of waste paper but when Chet unfolded it they regarded it with great respect.

Upon the paper, heavily inscribed in black ink, as though painted with a brush, were several Chinese characters.

"Gosh!" breathed Joe. "Chinese writing."

"Nothing else but," gloated Chet. "Now," he demanded triumphantly, "is that a clue or isn't it?"

"Maybe it's only a laundry check," said Frank dubiously. "It looks like one."

Chet was indignant.

"Now don't go turning my clue into a laundry check," he said. "That's a Chinese message. Boy, oh boy, I wish I had taken up Chinese when I was going to school. If we could only read this! I'll bet it's important."

Joe took the check and examined it carefully.

"Three collars, four shirts and a pair of socks," he translated.

Chet snatched back the slip of paper.

"Collars and socks, my neck!" he said. "It's probably a message announcing a revolution in China or something. Don't you see what it means? Why, it *proves* Aunt Gertrude wasn't dreaming last night. It's certain there was a Chinaman in the house. He left those footprints under the window and he dropped that message from his pocket.''

"I think it may be a valuable clue, all right," admitted Frank. "We'll have to find out what it means."

Just then they saw a stout, pleasant-faced woman coming up the front walk.

"This must be the nurse," said Frank. The boys went around to the front of the house to meet her.

"Were you sent by Dr. Bates?" inquired Joe politely.

"I was," replied the woman. "My name is Mrs. Cody, and I'm a nurse. If you'll be good enough to show me into the house I'll get busy right away."

Her manner was rough but kind. Frank took the satchel and they escorted Mrs. Cody into the house.

"If there is anything you need—" began Joe.

"I'll ask for it, never fear," concluded the nurse, as she opened her satchel and took out a uniform and a cap. "Just show me to my room and leave the house to me. I understand your folks are away."

The boys showed her upstairs, ushered her to Aunt Gertrude's room, and then departed.

"That's a relief," remarked Joe as they went downstairs. "Aunt Gertrude is in good hands, at any rate."

"So are you and Joe," reminded Chet. "You'll have to toe the mark now."

He took from his pocket the slip of paper he had found beneath the bushes.

"What are we going to do about this?"

"I wish Sam Lee hadn't gone away," said Frank. "He would have translated that for us in a second."

Joe suggested that they take the paper to Sam Lee's successor at the laundry, but the other boys did not approve of the idea.

"Take it to Louie Fong?" snorted Chet. "Not me. I don't like that rascal. He'd probably tell us something that wasn't on the note at all."

"I don't trust him myself," Frank agreed. "We'd better look around for a more dependable Chinaman."

Joe suggested that they go down to the docks. He still felt that they might be able to trace the missing Sidney Pebbles.

"Don't you remember?" he said. "Pebbles spoke to a Chinaman after he got off the boat. And there were a number of others hanging around the dock at the time. The whole affair may be connected with that fight early this morning."

"And what a fight it was!" exclaimed Chet. "If the police hadn't shown up in time there would have been corpses all over the place."

Frank asked him if the police had learned the reason for the fight but Chet said that the injured Chinaman, who had been taken to the hospital in the neighboring town of Lakeside, had refused to talk.

"They're a secretive crowd," he said, "They like to settle their little quarrels in their own way without getting mixed up with the law. I doubt if the police will ever know just why that battle began."

The others agreed that they might pick up some information by visiting the scene of the fight. It would do no harm, at any rate, to inquire about Sidney Pebbles at the steamship office. He might have left Bayport by an early morning boat.

Satisfied that Aunt Gertrude was in good hands they felt free to leave the house. Chet armed himself with several apples and stuffed a few biscuits into his pockets in case he should be overcome by hunger in the course of the morning.

As they drew near the corner laundry where the sign of Sam Lee still swung over the door, Frank remarked that it would do no harm to remind Louie Fong of the laundry they had left with him the previous afternoon.

"He might have it ready for us today after all," suggested Joe.

The door of the shop was closed. This was

unusual, because the day was warm. Frank
tried the door, but it was locked. There was
no sign of life around the place.

"That's queer," he said. "I never heard of
a laundry closing up in the middle of the
week."

"I guess you'd better say goodbye to all
your shirts," said Chet.

It was evident that the place was deserted.
Louie Fong might be merely taking a day's
holiday or he might have closed up the place
and departed from Bayport forever. There
was no notice on the door to indicate the reason for this sudden cessation of business.

"That's a fine kettle of fish," said Chet Morton. "Chinaman fightee at night. Closee
laundlee next day. This whole business gets
mysteriouser and mysteriouser."

As no good would be served by staring at
the locked door, the boys moved on. Inside
of a few minutes they were within sight of the
docks.

"I wonder what we'll learn here," said Joe.

Chet took an apple from his pocket, polished
it on his sleeve, and destroyed half of it at one
bite.

"Probably nothing," he mumbled.

But he was wrong.

# CHAPTER VII

## A MESSAGE FROM HOME

CONSTABLE CON RILEY was an important man that morning. As he strode solemnly back and forth on the steamship dock he represented the law in all its majesty. Also, he represented Information. Everyone who came to the wharf that day stopped to get a first-hand account of the dramatic doings of the previous night. News of the fight among the Chinamen had spread swiftly throughout Bayport.

Riley, his hands clasped behind his back, his chest out and his chin in the air, was even more dignified than usual. He was a very diligent constable, was Riley—a diligent man who took himself seriously. The unfortunate fact that he was so thick-headed had made him the despair of his superiors.

He had been a patrolman on a downtown beat but a pickpocket had stolen his handcuffs and nightstick. So Constable Con Riley had been placed on traffic duty, where nobody could steal anything from him.

On traffic duty he had given the Mayor of

Bayport a ticket without that gentleman deserving one. The Mayor had taken the matter up with the Chief, and as a result the worthy Riley had been transferred to the docks, where it was assumed that he could do no possible harm.

When he saw the Hardy boys and Chet Morton approaching him this morning he frowned. He knew them of old. Chet Morton had knocked off his helmet with a snowball the previous winter. The Hardy boys had solved some of his best cases before he could get really started on them and had made him look foolish more than once.

"Good morning, Mr. Riley," the trio said sweetly.

"Mornin'. Mornin'," grunted the policeman, with the air of a man with weighty problems on his mind.

"I hear you broke up a big fight last night, Constable," said Chet.

Riley glanced at him suspiciously. Chet had a reputation as a jokesmith.

"Well now, and I wouldn't say I exactly broke up the fight," said Riley. "As a matter of fact, I was home in bed. I ain't on night duty. But if I *had* been here," he declared pompously, "that fight would have been busted up a lot sooner than it was, let me tell you."

"You missed the fight?" said Joe. "That's

too bad. We came down because we thought you'd be able to tell us all about it."

"Well!" said Riley. "And can't you ask me? Just because I wasn't here—worse luck— doesn't mean I don't know all the details."

"We're in luck, fellows," said Chet. "Constable Riley is going to tell us the details. You didn't get here until it was all over, did you, Constable?"

"None of your cheek, now," said Riley. "I didn't get here until this mornin', because I'm on day duty as I said."

"I'll bet you were glad of that. What with people being stabbed and dumped into the water it wouldn't have been very comfortable on night duty," said Chet. Frank nudged him to be quiet.

"From what I can learn," said Riley with a severe glance at Chet, "the whole business was a food."

"A what?" said Frank, puzzled.

"A food. One of them foods among Chinamen. You know."

"Like chop suey?" inquired Chet, interested.

"A food, I said," declared Riley. "A battle. A war. A food."

"A feud!" exclaimed Joe.

"What were they fighting about?" asked Chet.

"Nobody knows," Riley replied. "The way

this here battle last night started, it seems there were some Chinamen down here on the dock waitin' for the boat to come in. You were here, I remember.''

"We saw them," said Frank.

"Well, I went off duty at midnight and they were still here. Still hangin' around. Said they were just waitin' for *another* boat to come in. I had no fault to find with that, so I went."

"Just in time," murmured Chet.

"And the minute I'm out of the way, trouble starts, of course. Another Chinaman came down to the dock and picked a quarrel with one of the fellows who was here already. So then he went away——"

"Which Chinaman?" asked Chet.

"The second Chinaman."

"Which one was that? The one who was here first?"

"No," spluttered Riley. "The second Chinaman was the one who had the row with the first Chinaman. He got here second."

"The first one?"

Constable Riley flushed.

"I'm tellin' this story," he said darkly. "The second Chinaman went away but along about three o'clock in the morning he came back with some more Chinamen."

"And the others were still here?"

"Still here. Still waitin' for *another* boat,

they said. And when the other Chinamen
landed here it wasn't two shakes of a lamb's
tail before they were fightin' like cats.

"They were fightin' all over the place and
the night man in the steamship office put in a
call for the police but it was all over before
they could get here. One Chinaman was lyin'
on the dock with a knife in him, and another
was swimmin' around in the water, half
drowned. So they pulled the one out and sent
the other to the hospital and not a word can
they get out of him about how it happened or
who done it."

"Who did it," corrected Chet.

"That's what they can't find out," exploded
Riley. "I've just told you, you numbskull, that
he won't tell them who done it."

"Sorry. My hearing isn't what it used to be."

"It never was," growled Riley.

"What was the Chinaman's name?" asked
Frank.

"Tom Wat."

"Tom Wat!" exclaimed Joe. "Why, we
know him. He works in that restaurant down
on Pine Street. At least, he used to work there.
Quiet little fellow."

"Well," grunted Riley, "he was mighty
nearly quieted for good."

"And none of the Chinamen were arrested?"
asked Joe.

"They were all gone except the man in the water and the lad with the knife in his shoulder," said Riley. "You can't arrest a man for swimmin' around the dock at three o'clock in the morning, or for gettin' a knife stuck in him, can you?"

"It would be most unjust," agreed Chet solemnly.

Having received this account of the battle, the boys thanked Constable Riley warmly and went on over to the ticket office of the steamship company. They knew the agent in charge.

"Hello, fellows," he said breezily, when they came up to the window. "What can I do for you? Where do you want to go? New York, Boston, Halifax, New Orleans, Cuba, Bermuda——"

"Week-end jaunt to China will do me," said Chet.

"Don't talk about China," said the agent. "I've heard enough about the Chinese today to last me a lifetime."

"Were you on duty during the row last night?" asked Frank.

"No, I was home and in bed, thank goodness."

"Then you wouldn't know if a young man named Pebbles left Bayport on the two-thirty boat?"

"I wasn't here, but I know he didn't. The

night man told me no one left Bayport on that boat. He might have gone on one of the steamers this morning, though. What does he look like?"

The boys described Sidney Pebbles to the best of their ability. The agent shook his head.

"He didn't show up here this morning. That is, he didn't buy a ticket."

The result of their inquiry had been unsatisfactory. They knew that Sidney Pebbles had not bought a boat ticket, but that he might have left Bayport by steamer just the same.

"What's the idea?" asked the agent curiously. "Doing some detective work?"

"We were just wondering where he had gone," replied Frank evasively.

"I could ask the boat captains. What's the name again? Pebbles. They might remember."

They thanked the agent and drifted disconsolately out of the office. Constable Riley was standing at the edge of the dock contemplating the horizon.

They heard the strident honk of an automobile horn. With a crash and a roar a car shot down from the roadway onto the dock. Constable Riley jumped and nearly toppled into the water. The ancient vehicle skidded and jolted to a stop.

At the wheel was Jerry Gilroy, and wedged

in the seat beside him were Phil Cohen and Tony Prito. All three were chums of Chet Morton and the Hardy boys.

"Call for the Hardy boys! Call for the Hardy boys!" chanted the trio, as the old car steamed and trembled as if on the verge of a complete breakdown.

"What's the matter?" asked Frank.

"You're wanted at home," said Tony Prito.

"We called around to see you and a nurse said to look you up and tell you that you were wanted at home right away," explained Phil.

"We got scared," Jerry explained, "when we saw the nurse. Is someone ill?"

"I thought your folks were all away," added Tony with concern.

"She didn't say who was ill," said Phil, referring to the attendant, "but she said excitedly, 'Find Joe and Frank and bring them home at once!'"

"I stepped on the gas, and believe me, we've been doing some speeding," exclaimed Jerry. "Glad we found you. Hop in!"

The Hardy boys scrambled into the rear seat, and the old auto gave a great leap as the driver let in the clutch. Joe and Frank looked at each other, worry written on their faces.

"Goodnight!" gasped Joe. "I hope nothing more has happened to Aunt Gertrude!"

# CHAPTER VIII

## ORRIN NORTH'S STORY

JERRY GILROY'S venerable junk-heap broke its own speed record that morning after the Hardy boys had jumped into the rear seat. With a tremendous uproar of back-firing and clatter of loose mudguards it jolted back up High Street.

Both Frank and Joe were alarmed over the news they had received. Their first thought was that Aunt Gertrude had taken a turn for the worse. They reflected wretchedly that they should not have left the house at all. When the car reached the house they hastily bade goodbye to their chums, leaped out of the car and rushed up the walk.

However, when they ran into the hall they found Mrs. Cody emerging placidly from the living room.

"How is she?" gasped Frank.

"Your aunt?" said Mrs. Cody. "Oh, she's sleepin' as peaceful as a lamb. Don't worry your heads about her as long as I'm here."

"Then why did you send for us?"

Mrs. Cody looked blankly at them through her spectacles.

"I *did* send for you, didn't I?" she said.

"Yes. Why did you want us?" asked Frank.

"I'm blessed if I can remember," she said simply. "I know there was *something,* but it seems to have slipped my mind. Let me see——"

The good woman pursed her lips, tapped her chin with her forefinger and stared intently at the ceiling as she tried to remember why she had sent the urgent message. She was prompted by an impatient cough that sounded sharply from beyond the drawing-room door.

"Oh, yes!" she exclaimed. "I remember now. If he hadn't coughed I declare I think I'd have forgotten all about him. There's a man in there. He wants to see you," and, greatly pleased with herself at this triumph of memory, Mrs. Cody went on upstairs.

When Frank and Joe went into the drawing-room they found a highly excited and greatly agitated man awaiting them. They recognized him as Orrin North, a wealthy steamship owner who lived in Lakeside not far from Bayport.

Orrin North was a big, burly, broad-shouldered man with a coarse, red face, clumsy hands and a stubborn, obstinate chin. He was fond of saying that he was a self-made man for he had risen to power and wealth by his own efforts. A fisherman's son, he had worked hard and long until he had bought a boat of his own. From that, by his own ruthless efforts, he had gained control of a small fleet of vessels. In the course of years he had become wealthier and it had been hinted that not all his riches had been honestly earned. In middle life he had bought the fleet of a bankrupt trading company, and by business methods which were not above a suspicion of shadiness he had throttled competition and added to his fleet until he was now one of the most powerful men in the state.

This was the man, then, who sat impatiently in the Hardy home. Frank and Joe were so astonished that they could scarcely speak.

"Are you Fenton Hardy's sons?"

"Yes, Sir," said Frank.

"My name's North. Orrin North. Where is your father?"

"He is on a trip just now, Mr. North," said Frank. "We really don't know just where he is."

The man muttered something under his breath. He brought a huge fist crashing down upon the table.

"I've got to get in touch with him," he rasped. "Right away."

"I'm afraid that's impossible."

"It ain't impossible," roared North in an ugly manner. "Don't tell me your father didn't leave his address. You can reach him if you want to. Tell him Orrin North wants him back in Bayport at once."

The boys did not like their caller's domineering manner. They had heard many stories of his cruel, scheming and unscrupulous nature.

"I have told you the truth, Mr. North," said Frank calmly.

The man rose suddenly from his chair and strode nervously about the room.

"I've got to see him!" he shouted. "Do you hear? I've got to see him at once. It's important. I can't be kept waiting like this. I'm not used to it."

Frank shrugged.

"We don't know where our father is. Unless you can locate him yourself I'm afraid you'll just have to wait."

North glared at him.

"So! I'll have to wait, eh? Well, let me tell you this, young feller. Orrin North don't wait for nobody."

"Perhaps," suggested Joe mildly, "if you'll explain your business we may be able to help you."

The shipowner laughed contemptuously.

"You!" he said. "A couple of boys! I don't tell my business to babies."

"In that case," observed Frank acidly, "you are wasting your time talking to us. Good morning, Mr. North."

He opened the drawing-room door as if to show the burly visitor out. At once Orrin North became calmer.

"Don't be in such a rush," he said. "Mebbe i spoke a little too fast. After all—" he sat down again, "after all," he muttered, "you may be able to help me."

"We'll be glad to do what we can," Frank assured him.

North grunted doubtfully. "You're sure your father isn't in Bayport?" he said.

"I imagine we would know about it if he came back," smiled Joe.

"Then how," roared North, "does it happen that I got those papers in the second mail this morning with a Bayport postmark on the envelope? How does it happen? Answer me that!"

"What papers?" asked Frank.

North drew a bulky envelope from his pocket and tapped it with a stubby forefinger.

"These! Papers in an important case your pa is handling for me. Every one of 'em came back to me this morning. In the second mail. If your pa didn't send 'em, then who did? And why?"

Frank and Joe looked at each other. Papers!

Mailed in Bayport! Instantly their minds
flashed to the papers missing from Fenton
Hardy's pockets.

"Why, that's strange," said Frank. "We
had a burglary here last night and some of
Dad's papers were stolen. Those may have
been among them."

"But no one knew about these papers,"
roared North. "I gave them to your father
on the quiet."

"And they were mailed to you this
morning?"

"You heard me," growled North.

He thrust the envelope over to Frank.
"Look at that," he said, indicating the address and the postmark. "Mailed here in Bayport. To my address in Lakeside."

Eagerly the boys examined the envelope.
The address was typewritten. The postmark
showed that the letter had been mailed in Bayport at eight o'clock that morning. It would
reach Lakeside in the second morning mail, as
Orrin North had said.

"Perhaps this throws some light on the
burglary," mused Frank. "These must be the
stolen papers. But why would Sidney Pebbles——"

"Who?" shouted Orrin North, his face dark
with anger and astonishment.

"Do you know him?" asked Frank quickly.

"Sidney Pebbles? I should say I do know him. But what has he to do with this?"

"He stayed here last night as our guest," Joe explained. "We met him down at the dock and he missed his boat so we asked him to spend the night here. When we woke up this morning we found he had disappeared. And papers were missing from Dad's pockets."

"Sidney Pebbles—stayed here—ran away—papers missing—" stammered North. "I don't believe it."

"What do you know about Pebbles?"

"I don't know much about him," declared North, "but I'm sure he ain't a crook. Not that young feller. He works in Lakeside. I've seen him often."

"Works in Lakeside?" exclaimed the Hardy boys. Nothing that Sidney Pebbles had said on the previous night had indicated that he lived anywhere near Bayport.

"Sure. He works at a roadhouse up the river. Chinese joint."

This was another shock. It seemed to fit in neatly with the other pieces of the jigsaw puzzle the mystery presented. The boys were greatly excited now. They were positive that some sinister connection existed between Sidney Pebbles and the Chinamen on the dock.

"But nobody can ever tell me that Sidney Pebbles swiped them papers," declared Orrin

North firmly. "I don't know the feller real well but I'm sure he ain't a crook. Besides, there wouldn't be no sense to it. Why would he steal them papers and mail them to me? And how would he know about 'em in the first place?"

"On the other hand," Frank pointed out, "we know he was here and we know he cleared out of the house before we were up and we know that the papers are missing from the guest room. Someone left footprints underneath one of the downstairs windows, too."

"They weren't Pebbles's footprints, then," grunted North. "I don't believe he had anything to do with it. Anyway, I don't care. The papers ain't stolen. I've got 'em right here. The point is this: What am I goin' to do with 'em? They're mighty important and I gave 'em to your pa so he could handle this big case for me. What am I goin' to do? Wait till your pa comes back? Turn the papers over to somebody else? I'm left stranded."

"I think," said Frank, "that you'd better wait until Dad comes back."

"I can't wait," howled North.

"In that case perhaps you'd better turn the case over to someone else. If Dad left the papers in one of his coat pockets it must have meant that he couldn't handle the affair until he came back from his trip, anyway."

"There's sense to that," grunted North.

"But we'd like to find out why Pebbles took them—if he did take them."

"I'll fix him if he took 'em. I'll have him fired from his job. I'll have him thrown into jail. If he knows what's in them papers——"

A sudden thought evidently flashed through Orrin North's mind for his eyes glowed with a dangerous light. His fists clenched.

"If he knows what's in them papers and means to try and gouge some money out of me," he rasped, "he'll wish he'd picked on somebody else. He'll wish he'd never been born!"

The shipowner snatched up the envelope and thrust it back into his pocket. Then he grabbed his hat from the table. He was an ugly, formidable figure as he towered above the boys in the room.

"Nobody plays them games on Orrin North and gets away with 'em," he snarled. "I've crushed too many men in my time."

"Where can we find Sidney Pebbles?" asked Frank.

"Come to Lakeside. Come to my office tomorrow and I'll tell you where to find him," said North. "If it's the same man—which I doubt—we'll settle up with him. My office at ten o'clock."

"We'll be there," they promised.

"All right. And if you have any word from your father, give me a call on the telephone."

Orrin North jammed his hat down about his ears, picked up his heavy stick and strode out of the room. The boys showed him the way out, and with a muttered word of goodbye he clumped off down the walk.

CHAPTER IX

## LOUIE FONG IS ANGRY

ALTHOUGH the Hardy boys felt that they had
made great progress in the mystery by reason
of the important news they had learned from
Orrin North, they were more puzzled than ever
when the shipowner left them.

"I can't understand why a man should steal
papers and mail them right back to the owner,"
said Joe. "It seems a crazy stunt to me."

"It may not be as crazy as it looks," re-
joined his brother. "Maybe Sidney Pebbles is
a blackmailer. For all we know, there may be
information in those papers that might hurt
Orrin North. Remember, he said he gave them
to Dad on the quiet. They were confidential.
Once the papers were mailed back to the owner
no one could prove that Pebbles stole them.
And if he read them he would have the information and he might try to blackmail North
on the strength of it."

"Mr. North suggested something of the sort
himself."

"That may be the explanation of the whole

affair. Yet it's strange that Mr. North seems so sure that the Sidney Pebbles he knows can't be the thief.''

''Well,'' Joe said, ''for that matter we're not sure that the Sidney Pebbles *we* know was the thief. If he didn't make those footprints under the window, then there was someone else.''

''It's enough to make a fellow's head swim,'' Frank remarked. ''We should know more about it tomorrow. Odd, isn't it, that this fellow Pebbles works at a Chinese place?''

''It all seems to come back to Chinamen every time,'' his brother admitted.

The boys made no further progress on the case that day, nor were they successful in their efforts to locate Mr. and Mrs. Hardy. They sent several messages to places where they understood their parents were to stop, but had received no replies as yet.

Dr. Bates called that evening to see Aunt Gertrude, who was still weak and ill but had been resting well and had shown some improvement under the care of Mrs. Cody. That motherly lady had taken full charge of the house and the boys were spared the bother of preparing meals. What was more, they escaped the toil of washing dishes.

''Clear out of my kitchen,'' she ordered cheerfully when they offered to help. ''I'm running this house until your aunt is on her feet again, poor darlin'. Just let me manage things my own way and we'll all be satisfied."

"It suits me," declared Joe, "right down to the ground."

"There's something I meant to ask you," she said. "Where are all the fresh towels and pillow-slips and the like?"

"They're at the laundry," the boys told her. "They would have been ready today but there's a new laundryman on the job and he isn't very obliging. Besides, his place was closed today."

"If you don't get them tomorrow," said Mrs. Cody grimly, "tell me, and I'll fix him."

She sat down at the kitchen table and began to read her fortune in the tea-leaves in her cup. It appeared that Mrs. Cody was superstitious and that she firmly believed that the future could be foretold by this method. She giggled delightedly as she informed the boys that the cup promised her that she would be invited to a big party within the week and that there was to be a parcel in the mail for her within the next few days.

Then she frowned.

"What's this? What's this?" muttered the good woman. "Trouble, as sure as you're born. Oh, mercy, why did I have to read my cup this night? There's enough trouble without knowing about it before it comes."

"What kind of trouble is it to be, Mrs.

Cody?'' asked Frank, who did not believe in
teacup reading.

She turned the cup to the light.

"There's a letter C here," said Mrs. Cody
tensely. "You can notice it as plain as day.
Now what could that mean? Trouble dealin'
with the letter C? And it's hangin' right over
us. My, my—I don't like this at all, at all."

"Chinamen," muttered Joe.

"What's that?" asked Mrs. Cody.

"Nothing," said Joe, and they made their
escape from the kitchen.

"I wonder if there is anything in this for-
tune-telling stuff after all?" said Frank, as
they were preparing for bed.

"If trouble is going to come it will come,
and that's all there is to it," replied Joe
philosophically. "We just have to be ready
for it."

Next morning after breakfast they set out
for Louie Fong's laundry for the purpose of
claiming the week's washing. They had determined, if they found the place still closed,
to report the matter to the police.

But there was no need of that. The establishment was a scene of thriving activity.
Steam issued in a cloud from the front door,
and when the boys stepped inside the evil face
of Louie Fong popped up from behind the
counter like a jack-in-the-box.

"Hullo! You come fo' laundly. No got,"
he said sharply.

"What's the idea?" demanded Frank.

"Solly. No got. Tomolla, mebbe."

"Tomorrow! That's another day lost,"
complained Joe. "Why weren't you working
yesterday? That's why we can't have our
laundry today."

"No work yes'day," said Louie Fong. "Beeg
Chinese hol'day."

The Hardy boys doubted this. Sam Lee had
always given notice when he intended to ob-
serve a holiday, and they could not recall that
he had ever closed his laundry in the middle of
summer.

"All right," sighed Frank. He leaned
against the counter, in no hurry to leave. "You
didn't close up on account of the battle down
on the docks, did you?"

"Beeg fight, eh? Fella get stab. Good. He
look fo' tlouble."

"Did you know the man who got stabbed,
Tom Wat? How is he getting along?"

"In hospital. Him get all betta soon.
Too bad."

"Too bad he got hurt?"

"No. Too bad he get all betta," said
Louie Fong unsympathetically. "He look fo'
tlouble."

"How was he looking for trouble?"

Louie Fong's eyes narrowed suspiciously, and he did not reply.

Frank, while talking to the Chinaman, had noticed that alterations had been made in the laundry since he had last entered the place. Where he remembered a window to have been in the rear wall, there was now a door. The woodwork was new, and a partition had been erected at the back. In the middle of the floor he saw freshly painted wood that seemed to indicate the presence of a trapdoor. Why all these changes, he wondered. Perhaps these alterations explained the closing of the laundry on the previous day. He was sure that there were men behind the partition. There was not the usual cheerful bustle in the laundry and he saw no sign of Sam Lee's old helper.

But from beyond the partition came the sound of whispering, of an occasional rustle. He saw that Louie Fong's eyes darted toward the partition again and again. He also saw that the Chinaman was getting impatient, evidently waiting for them to leave.

"Where's Sam Lee now?" Joe inquired. "Any chance that he'll be coming back?"

"No wantee hear about Sam Lee!" shouted Louie Fong with sudden anger. "No talkee 'bout him. Gone away. No come back."

He was in a towering rage. His lanky, skinny hand pointed toward the door.

"Go 'way!" he ordered shrilly. "Why you come here and talkee, talkee, ask question? Laundly not leddy until tomolla. Go 'way. Come back tomolla."

"Oh, well," said Joe easily, "if that's the way you feel about it, we'll be on our way."

"Sure, and we'll be back tomorrow for the laundry," promised Frank.

"Go 'way! Go 'way!" screeched Louie Fong. He waved his arms wildly.

"Nice man," murmured Frank, when they were out on the street again. "He seems to rage whenever Sam Lee is mentioned."

"I hope he doesn't treat all his customers the same way," returned Joe. "He won't stay in business very long at that rate."

Frank was thinking of the alterations he had noticed in the laundry. He said thoughtfully:

"I have a notion that Louie Fong isn't depending entirely on the laundry business for a living."

"What do you mean?"

"Didn't you see all the carpentry work? That new partition and the extra door and the opening in the flooring? I'll bet that's why Louie closed the place up yesterday. He wanted to get the work done without being disturbed. Why should he make all those changes in a laundry? There's something queer about it."

"And I'm sure there was somebody behind the partition."

After talking it over the boys agreed that the temperamental Louie Fong would bear watching. The mysterious departure of honest old Sam Lee and the sudden change in the whole atmosphere of the place were circumstances that hinted at something shady and illegal.

As it was nearly time for their appointment with Orrin North in Lakeside, they went back to the house and took their roadster out of the garage. It was a big car that had seen better days. They had bought it while they were investigating a mysterious series of automobile thefts, as related in "The Shore Road Mystery" of this series, and since that time they had bought new parts and had repaired the engine until they now had a really serviceable car. In a few minutes they were speeding along the road to Lakeside.

"Now," said Frank, "for Mr. Sidney Pebbles."

"Perhaps this isn't the same Sidney."

"We'll soon find out. If he is *our* Sidney he will have a hard time explaining the disappearance of Mr. North's papers."

# CHAPTER X

WHEN the Hardy boys reached the office building of Orrin North's trading company they gave their names to a secretary.

"Mr. North is expecting you. Come this way, please."

He ushered them into a luxurious inner office where the boat owner sat writing at a mahogany desk. Orrin North looked up.

"Mornin', lads," he rumbled. "You're right on time. Well, I've fixed everything up."

"That's good, Sir," said Frank.

"You want to have a look at Sidney Pebbles. That's the first point. The second point is this: you don't want Sidney Pebbles to have a look at you."

The boys nodded in agreement. If this man was indeed the Sidney Pebbles who had been their guest they did not want to arouse his alarm until they were sure of his identity. Otherwise he might escape before they could have a chance of questioning him.

"It has to be done on the quiet," continued

North. "If he is really the same man we'll have a talk with him. If not, we'll leave him alone."

"How can we manage to see him without being seen?" asked Joe.

"I've fixed that," growled North. "Sidney Pebbles—*this* Sidney Pebbles—works at a place called 'Lantern Land,' just outside Lakeside. It's a roadhouse and eating place run by some Chinese people. Now, if we go out there we can hide in a little building just off the courtyard. It's used as a shelter for some of the chauffeurs on wet nights. We won't be seen and we can watch what's going on. We'll see Pebbles, because he acts as a sort of assistant manager around the place and he'll very likely be checking over the supplies that come to the restaurant in the morning."

"It seems to be a good plan," said Frank.

Orrin North sniffed.

"Sure it's a good plan. I thought it up myself," he said. "But somehow I got a feelin' you'll find that he ain't the man you want. I can't figure out why this Pebbles would want my papers. By the way, have you had any news of your pa?"

Frank shook his head.

"We tried to get in touch with him but we didn't have any luck."

North frowned.

"I wish he would come back. I don't know where I stand in this business."

He got up from his chair.

"Come along, then," he said. "You have a car here?"

"We came here in our roadster," Frank said.

"I'll lead the way in my own car. We'll park just outside the grounds."

Orrin North stepped into a sleek blue sedan at the door of the building and they started off. The boys followed him through the streets of Lakeside, out on a highway that paralleled the river. In about ten minutes they reached the grounds of the roadhouse. From the highway the building itself could not be seen for it was hidden by a grove of trees. There was a huge sign, however, at the entrance of the side road. It read: "Lantern Land—Food—Dancing."

North's car came to a stop. The boys drew the roadster up at the side of the road and stepped out.

"We'll walk up and then slip around to the back of the place through the trees," said their guide. "I fixed it up with one of the men working here. He's to leave the back door of the rest room open."

They trudged up the winding path. When they were within sight of the restaurant, a long white structure skirted by a wide veranda, they left the road and struck out beneath the trees until they circled the place and came in sight of a courtyard at the rear. There was no one in sight.

"Quickly, now!" commanded North.

He sped out from beneath the trees and strode swiftly toward a tiny white building at the side of the courtyard. The Hardy boys followed.

They reached the shelter without being observed. A large window gave them an unobstructed view of the entire courtyard. From the open windows of the roadhouse kitchen on the other side of the yard they could hear the clatter of dishes and the chatter of voices.

There was a rumble as a truck rolled into the courtyard. It came to a halt near the kitchen door and the driver stepped out of the cab. He began to unload baskets of fruit and vegetables. The kitchen door opened and a young man stepped out.

"That's him!" whispered North.

The boys watched the young man who came over to the truck. At first glance they were convinced that he was none other than the Sidney Pebbles who had stayed at their home and departed without waiting to say goodbye. He was the width of the courtyard away, however, and as he was inspecting the baskets and talking to the truck-driver the boys could not get a clear view of his face. They watched him as he signed a slip and went back into the road-house again.

"Well?" said North. "Is it the same fellow?"

"I couldn't be sure," admitted Frank. "He is of the same height and build but I didn't see his face very clearly. How about you, Joe?"

"At this distance I'd say he was the same Sidney Pebbles. But, like you, I didn't get a good glimpse of his face."

"You'd better make sure," grunted Orrin North. "We'll wait a while. He'll be out again."

The truck rumbled away. A Chinaman emerged from the kitchen, crossed the yard and disappeared through a doorway on the other side. After a while Sidney Pebbles came out again with a sheaf of papers in his hand. Whistling, he made his way to the entrance of the courtyard.

He passed directly in front of the window, and as he was hatless, the boys saw his face distinctly. The resemblance was startling. But he was not the Sidney Pebbles they had known.

His hair was darker in color. His eyes were darker. His mouth had a more determined expression. In many respects he was almost the double of the young man the Hardy boys had encountered on the dock—but he was not the same one.

Frank and Joe glanced at each other in open disappointment. Orrin North read their expressions.

"Not the same, eh?"

"I can't understand it," said Frank. "He looks *nearly* the same. It's almost impossible that there should be two men of the same name and looking so nearly alike."

"Unless he dyed his hair," ventured Joe.

"His hair ain't changed color since I first knew him," insisted North. "No, Sir, this can't be the same Sidney Pebbles."

Mr. North seemed to think the question was settled. The Hardy boys, however, were not quite satisfied. They wanted to hear the young man's voice. It seemed, as Frank had said, impossible that there should be two young men of identical names and almost identical appearance.

"I've heard of people havin' doubles," said Orrin North, "but I never yet heard of doubles havin' the same name."

"Perhaps our man was impersonating the real Sidney Pebbles," suggested Frank.

Orrin North pondered this idea for a moment.

"Might be something in it, at that."

At that moment a car rolled slowly into the

courtyard. It was a taxicab, which came to a
sudden stop, and the driver stepped out to open
the side door. A Chinaman emerged. He
clambered out of the car and took some money
from his pocket and paid the taxi driver. Then
he walked slowly over toward a side entrance,
limping slightly, as though the effort required
taxed his strength.

Through the window the boys had a glimpse
of his face. Frank uttered a gasp of astonishment, for he had recognized the Chinaman.

"Why, it's Tom Wat!" he exclaimed.

"Who?" demanded North. "What's his
name? Do you know him?"

"Tom Wat! The Chinaman who was stabbed
in the fight on the dock the night Sidney Pebbles disappeared."

They watched. The little Chinaman opened
a door and stepped inside. A moment later
Sidney Pebbles came running across the courtyard, and followed the wounded man through
the same doorway.

"Now why," asked Joe softly, "is Tom Wat
coming from the hospital to see Sidney Pebbles?"

"I think we'll stay around here for a while
and try to find out," returned his brother.

# CHAPTER XI

## TOM WAT'S ENEMIES

"You know this Chinaman?" asked Mr. North.

"We have seen him in Bayport," Frank told him. "There was a fight among Chinamen on the docks the night before last and he was stabbed. He was taken to the hospital in Lakeside."

"Queer business," muttered Orrin North. "What was the fight about?"

"No one knows but the Chinamen, and they won't talk about it. I'd like to speak to Tom Wat," said Frank.

"Well," said Orrin North, "I'm a busy man and I haven't time to waste. I've shown you Sidney Pebbles, so what do you want to do next?"

"I think we'd better stay and scout around a bit," decided Joe.

"Just as you like," returned the boat owner. "Your car is parked down by the road. I'm goin' back to my office."

He turned to leave.

"If you get any more news," said Mr. North gruffly, "or if you hear from your father, be sure to let me know."

"We will," they promised.

"All right, then. I'm on my way."

He left them, and a moment later they heard him striding through the undergrowth and shrubbery at the rear of the roadhouse.

"What now?" said Joe.

"What do you say to going right out and talking to this Sidney Pebbles? If some impostor is using his name he'll want to know about it."

But Joe was cautious.

"We'd better be careful," he said. "After all, we're not positive he isn't the Sidney Pebbles we know."

Just then the door of the side entrance opened, and Tom Wat, the Chinaman, hobbled out, with Sidney Pebbles holding him by the arm. The pair came down the steps and across the courtyard talking earnestly together. They went out to the yard gate, crossed the outer roadway and stood beneath a clump of trees.

"I wish we knew what they were talking about," said Joe.

"If we could get around behind those trees without being seen we might be able to listen."

The boys slipped out of the little rest room, stole around to the road, crossed it and made their way quietly through the bushes back of the roadhouse property. After a wide detour they heard a murmur of voices.

They advanced, scarcely making a sound. Soon they saw Tom Wat and Pebbles through the screen of leaves. Then they heard a voice.

"You say you just got out of the hospital a few minutes ago. What sent you there in the first place?"

"Me got hurt. One—two nights ago," replied Tom Wat. "Chinaboy try killee me."

"Tried to kill you?" asked Pebbles in surprise. "Why should anyone try to kill you?"

"Big fight," returned Tom Wat.

"But what was the fight about?"

"No savvy. Fella no likee me. Come up with big knife. I get hurt."

"And you don't know why you were stabbed?" asked Pebbles incredulously.

"Me gettee square," promised Tom Wat solemnly.

"You'll get square? With whom?"

"Louie Fong gang."

The Hardy boys started. So Louie Fong was involved in the battle on the wharf!

"What has Louie Fong been doing?" asked Pebbles. "How will you get square with him?"

"Land in jailee klick. Me tell police. Smuglee."

"You'll land him in jail for smuggling!"

There was a low whistle. "You'd better watch your step, that's all I can say. Well, let's get down to business. Why did you want to see me?" asked Pebbles.

"Why you come to dock in Bayport?"

"Why did I come to the dock in Bayport? When? What are you talking about?"

"Me see you. Night of fight. You come in on boat. You come back."

"You're crazy!" retorted Pebbles indignantly. "I haven't been in Bayport for a week. And I haven't been on a boat since last summer. Who told you all this?"

"Me, I see you!" exclaimed Tom Wat in excitement.

"You didn't see me. You couldn't have seen me. I've been working here at 'Lantern Land' every evening."

"You think mebbe me blindee in eye?" demanded Tom Wat. "Me see you on dock jus' befo' big fight start."

"You didn't see me on any dock before any fight started," declared Pebbles. "If that's why you came to see me you've picked the wrong man."

"Me see you on dock!"

"No you didn't. I'm not crazy enough to get myself mixed up in any Chinese feud. What makes you think I was there?"

"Samee fella," declared Tom Wat.

"Well, you're wrong, then. I haven't been in Bayport for a week. Ask any of the people who work here. They'll tell you the same."

Frank and Joe had crept closer. From the shelter of the trees they could plainly see Pebbles and the Chinaman. The white man seemed angry. As for Tom Wat, he was puzzled and confused, as if he did not know what to believe.

Suddenly the boys heard a blood-curdling snarl. Down the roadway streaked a gaunt, gray object. It was an enormous dog, lean and ferocious, with slavering jaws. It rushed toward the trees.

"Look out!" yelled Pebbles. "He's heading this way."

Tom Wat uttered a howl of terror and scrambled to one side. He grabbed a branch and tried to haul himself into the nearest tree. With a yelp and a snarl the animal left the road and leaped at Pebbles. The young man evaded the rush, however, by dodging behind a thick clump of bushes.

Frank and Joe were frozen with astonishment. At that moment the dog saw them.

The animal sprang, hurtling through the undergrowth. Frank and Joe scrambled desperately. All thought of concealment was gone. Snapping wickedly, the big brute crashed through the weeds and brush, close at their heels.

Behind them they could hear the shrill cries of the Chinaman, the shouts of Sidney Pebbles. The ferocious dog coursed madly in pursuit. Joe tripped over a branch and fell sprawling, but picked himself up in an instant and ran on.

The dog, however, had picked Frank as his prey, and was only a few feet behind. Although Frank was a good runner he knew he could not hope to shake off the animal's pursuit. He was hampered, too, by the undergrowth in his path.

Suddenly there was a howl of triumph. The lean body of the animal launched itself through the air, crashing heavily upon Frank's back. Boy and brute hurtled to the ground. Frank twisted, trying to protect his face and throat with one arm, while he battled to fight off the mad attacker.

Borne down by the weight of the maddened animal he was at a disadvantage. The infuriated beast slashed and tore savagely at his shoulder, and its sharp fangs sought the boy's throat.

Frank had uttered a shout as he was struck down. Joe heard it and turned. When he saw his brother knocked down by the maddened animal he looked swiftly about him for a weapon, and at his feet saw a heavy, knotted stick. He snatched it up and ran through the weeds to Frank's aid.

# CHAPTER XII

### THE CHINESE NOTE

IN SPITE of his struggles Frank might have been badly injured by the ferocious dog had it not been for Joe's timely arrival with the club.

*Crash!* The weapon came down upon the dog's head with all the force at Joe's command. The animal uttered a howl of rage and leaped back. It faced Joe, its bloodshot eyes glaring with hatred.

Joe sprang in again, swinging the club high. It struck the animal across the nose and drove the ugly dog back on its haunches. That was enough. The brute yelped in agony, wheeled, and scuttled off.

"Are you hurt?" asked Joe anxiously as his brother struggled to his feet.

Frank ruefully contemplated his torn and rumpled clothing.

"Not hurt at all," he said breathlessly. "But that doesn't mean you didn't do me a mighty good turn. I couldn't have fought that ugly brute off much longer. I wonder who owns the animal?"

Toward them ran Sidney Pebbles closely followed by the Chinaman. The latter was gabbling with excitement but Pebbles was quite calm. When he came up to the boys he said to Frank:

"You're lucky that brute didn't tear you to pieces, young fellow."

"I'd have been badly mauled if it hadn't been for my brother," admitted Frank.

"Just the same," continued Sidney Pebbles, "I can't say I'm sorry you got a lesson. Perhaps it will teach you not to go around spying on people."

At that moment Tom Wat came running up. When he saw the Hardy boys he recognized them at once.

"Ho!" he squealed. "Detective fella! Hide behin' tlees."

Pebbles swung around and faced the Chinaman squarely.

"What's that?" he demanded. "Detectives?"

"Sure!" exclaimed Tom Wat. "See um often in Bayport."

Sidney Pebbles thrust his hands into his pockets and faced the boys sternly.

"Look here," he said. "What's the idea? Who are you, anyway? You were hiding here in the bushes listening. What's it all about?"

"Me fixum!" declared Tom Wat shrilly.

"No likee spy. Mebbe Louie Fong sendum."

For the Hardy boys it was an awkward moment. They realized that Sidney Pebbles was quite justified in demanding an explanation. One thing was certain. This man was not the Sidney Pebbles they had met in Bayport. It was evident that he did not recognize them. There was only one thing to do, Frank decided, and that was to take the pair into their confidence.

"You don't know us, Mr. Pebbles?" he said.

"Know you? Of course I don't. I've never seen either of you before. And how do you know my name?"

"Didn't you meet us on the dock at Bayport two nights ago?" said Frank.

Pebbles was astonished. He looked first at Tom Wat, then at the boys.

"Say," he muttered, "I can't understand this. First of all the Chinaman says I was on the Bayport wharf the other night and now you two come along and say the same thing. What's behind it? Is this a joke? Why were you spying on me?"

"We were shadowing you for the same reason Tom Wat came here to see you," said Frank. "He thought you were the Sidney Pebbles who was on the dock at Bayport. So did we."

"Do you mean," demanded Pebbles angrily,

"that some fellow is going around using my name?"

"Not only your name but your face," grinned Joe. "He's your double. Your living image. Even yet I'm not sure you aren't the man."

Pebbles looked bewildered.

"I can't understand this at all," he said.

Frank turned to Tom Wat. The Chinaman, slender and slight of build, with a sallow, effeminate face, was staring intently at Pebbles.

"Is this the man you saw on the dock, Tom?"

Tom Wat shook his head slowly.

"One time me thinkee yes," he said. "Now me thinkee no. Him difflent."

"Why did you come here to see Mr. Pebbles?"

"Me meetum fella on dockee at Baypo't," explained Tom Wat. "He tellee me he savvy all 'bout Louie Fong gang. 'What your name?' I askee him. 'Pebbles,' him say. 'Sidney Pebbles.' Big fightee start. Me gettum hurt. Docto' man tellum Sidney Pebbles wo'ks at Lanteln Land."

"So you came out here to see him and ask him what he knew about Louie Fong's gang?" said Frank.

Sidney Pebbles shrugged his shoulders helplessly.

"It's too deep for me," he said. "I don't know this Louie Fong. Never heard of him.

I wasn't on the dock at Bayport. I don't know anything about it."

"It's simply a case of mistaken identity," said Joe. "We have been trying to find this other Sidney Pebbles and we heard that a man by that name worked here. We made the same mistake Tom Wat did."

"I hope he doesn't go around robbing any banks," said Pebbles. "If this fellow looks like me and uses my name I may find myself booked for a penitentiary term. Why are you fellows so eager to lay your hands on him? Tom Wat says you are detectives."

Frank explained that they were the sons of Fenton Hardy. He told how they had encountered the other Sidney Pebbles on the dock, how they had taken him to their home and how he had disappeared.

"And at the same time," he concluded, "some of my father's valuable papers disappeared, too."

Sidney Pebbles groaned.

"This namesake is going to get me into trouble," he said seriously.

"What's all this trouble about the Louie Fong gang?" asked Joe, turning to the Chinaman.

Tom Wat's face suddenly became expressionless.

"No savvy!"

"Sure, you understand. Are you a friend of Louie Fong?"

An expression of hatred flickered across the man's smooth face.

"Me hatee Louie Fong!"

"You hate him. Why?"

The Chinaman shrugged. He was not disposed to tell too much.

"Is there a feud between Louie Fong's gang and your crowd?"

"Mebbe," returned the Chinaman non-committally.

"What started the fight on the dock?"

"No savvy."

The boys saw that they were not going to get much information from Tom Wat.

"What I'd like to know," grumbled Sidney Pebbles, "is where that dog came from?"

"Doesn't he belong to you?" asked Frank.

"Never saw him before. Looked like a Russian wolfhound to me. It's the first time I've ever seen the brute around Lantern Land."

"That's another queer angle," remarked Joe. "The dog came as if somebody had set him on us."

"Dog come afte' me," said Tom Wat suddenly.

"He came after you? Why?"

"No savvy," returned the Chinaman promptly.

"I wish you'd tell us more about this whole affair, Tom," said Frank. "We're trying to help you. We don't like Louie Fong any more than you do. What brings him to Bayport anyway? Where is Sam Lee?"

Tom Wat shrugged again.

"He's going to tell us he doesn't savvy," grunted Joe in disgust.

"No savvy," said Tom Wat, running true to form.

"Might as well talk to a stone wall," observed Pebbles. "You won't get anything out of him, that's certain."

"This other Pebbles told you he knew something about Louie Fong's gang," persisted Frank. "Did he tell you anything else?"

Tom Wat shook his head.

Suddenly Joe had an inspiration.

"I suppose you can read Chinese writing," he said.

Tom Wat blinked.

"Sometime," he replied cautiously.

Joe rummaged in his pockets for the note he had found beneath the bushes near the window of the Hardy home. He found it, unfolded it and handed it to the Chinaman.

"Can you read that?"

Tom Wat took the note, and studied it carefully. Then his expression changed, as he muttered a few excited words in Chinese.

"Where you getee this?" he demanded quickly.

"We found it after Sidney Pebbles had cleared out of our house. It was under the bushes, near some footprints."

The Chinaman muttered to himself, studying the note again.

"You watchee you' step!" he exclaimed. "Bad fella at you' house. Dlop this note."

"A bad fellow dropped that note. Who was he? What does it say?"

"Plenty tlouble," grunted Tom Wat.

Sidney Pebbles became exasperated.

"Well!" he exclaimed. "Tell us what the note says."

# CHAPTER XIII

## THE KNIFE

At first Tom Wat was not inclined to translate the note. With loyalty to his race he did not want to explain anything to the white boys.

But Frank and Joe insisted. Sidney Pebbles bullied him a little.

"Read it," the latter snapped. "It isn't your note."

Tom Wat sighed.

"Note say Misteh Ha'dy make no plogless on Nolth case."

"Mr. Hardy is making no progress on the North case!" exclaimed Frank, astonished. "Are you sure that's what it said?"

"You thinkee me lie, you lead note you'self," said Tom Wat.

"No, I don't think you're lying. I was only surprised. Is that all that's written there?"

Tom Wat looked at the note again.

"Him say Misteh Ha'dy is out of town. It is time to stlike."

"Time to strike!" gasped Joe. "What does that mean?"

Tom Wat shrugged.

"Time to strike!" repeated Frank. "I don't like that."

"Sounds like trouble," agreed Sidney Pebbles seriously. "What do you think it means?"

"Dad has been working on a case for Orrin North," Joe explained. "I can't imagine why any Chinaman should be interested, however."

"Some Chinaman is very much interested, that's clear," declared Pebbles. "I'd advise you chaps to be on your guard."

"Against whom?" said Joe.

"That's the question. You don't know what it's all about."

"Bad fella," grunted Tom Wat suddenly. He thrust the note out and pointed to a tiny mark in ink in the lower left-hand corner.

"What does that mean?" asked Frank.

"Me savvy," said Tom mysteriously. "Bad fella come your place."

"I wish we knew what case our father was working on for Mr. North," muttered Joe. "We're quite in the dark now."

"Mr. North won't tell you?" suggested Pebbles.

"I hardly think so. He didn't volunteer any information anyway. When this other Pebbles disappeared from our house some papers vanished at the same time and I think they were information in the North case."

"Then he took them," said Pebbles decisively.

"We're not sure." Joe explained further about Aunt Gertrude's dream about the Chinaman, and the circumstances of the strange footprints under the window.

"This note opens up a new angle, you see. Aunt Gertrude may not have been dreaming. There may have been a *real* Chinaman in the house."

Sidney Pebbles whistled softly.

"It's too deep for me," he admitted.

At that moment there was a startling interruption. A curious rustling among the leaves of the trees was followed by a whirring sound. Something bright and gleaming flashed in the sun. Tom Wat uttered a startled cry, and leaped back, just as a gleaming object whizzed through the air and buried itself in the ground at his feet.

For a moment the boys were dumbfounded. Then Frank sprang forward, snatching up the object quivering in the earth. It was a knife, a long, sharp, evil-looking knife. Had Tom Wat failed to leap back in the nick of time the blade would have struck him with terrific force.

"Who threw that?" shouted Sidney Pebbles.

Tom Wat was white with fear. He could not speak. With a trembling finger he pointed toward the bushes. Frank and Joe wheeled and sprang toward the shrubbery. They crashed into the undergrowth in the direction from which the knife had come, and caught sight of a darting shadow among the trees.

"After him!" he shouted.

The shadow vanished as swiftly and as mysteriously as it had appeared. Though the boys ran toward the place with all possible speed, they found no one.

"Go that way, Joe!" urged Frank, gesturing toward the left. "I'll take this side of the bush. We'll get him, but be careful."

They separated and went crashing through the heavy growth. In the distance Frank heard the quick snapping of twigs, and followed the sound. He emerged upon a narrow trail, at the end of which was a tiny clearing.

The opening, for the moment, was deserted. Then, out of the dense screen of leaves, emerged a man. He came out quite silently. Scarcely a branch stirred in his wake. He sped across the space, plunged into the bushes on the other side and was gone.

Frank had no more than a fleeting glimpse of his yellow, evil face, but that was enough.

"Louie Fong!" he gasped.

He ran down the trail and entered the clearing. There he paused and listened, hoping to hear some sound of the fugitive's flight. He heard nothing but a great crashing in the

bushes about a hundred yards away, indicating
the presence of Joe.

Frank thrust aside the undergrowth where
he had last seen the Chinaman, and followed,
but he heard no further sound. He searched
the bushes thoroughly. After a while he was
joined by his brother.

"Can't find a sign of him," panted Joe.

"I saw him," said Frank. "He was too
quick for me, though. I think we've lost him."

"You saw him! Would you know him again?
What did he look like?"

"It was Louie Fong!"

Joe was astounded.

"Are you sure?"

"Louie Fong or his double. I caught only
a glimpse of him but I don't think I'm mistaken."

The boys resumed their search, but after ten
minutes' fruitless hunt through the brush they
were obliged to admit defeat. Louie Fong—if
it had really been the Chinaman—had given
them the slip.

They returned to the place where they had
left Tom Wat and Sidney Pebbles. The
former was shaking with fear. His face was
gray. He was frankly terrified. His narrow
escape from death had left him completely
shaken and unnerved.

"Boy!" exclaimed Pebbles. "Another inch

and we'd have had a corpse on our hands. Couldn't you catch the fellow?"

Frank shook his head.

"I saw him but he got away."

Tom Wat clutched eagerly at his sleeve.

"You see him? Who?"

"I think it was Louie Fong."

Tom Wat groaned. He covered his face with his trembling hands.

"No good. No good," he muttered. "Allee samee dead man now."

"You're not dead yet," said Pebbles. "Do you mean to say this Louie Fong is trying to kill you?"

"Almost killee me on dock," moaned Tom Wat. "Next time him makee sure."

"But why?" demanded Frank. "What has Louie Fong against you?"

"No can talk. Him enemy. Him killee me next time. Shut me up."

"He is going to kill you to shut you up so you won't talk any more?"

Tom Wat nodded, trembling.

Sidney Pebbles shrugged his shoulders.

"That's nonsense. Go tell the police. Tell them he threw a knife at you. They'll fix him in a hurry."

"Louie Fong in jailee, me die allee samee. Louie Fong man come 'long some night. Tom Wat die."

The little Chinaman seemed convinced that there was no hope for him. Even Louie Fong's arrest would not save him from revenge and death at the hands of the leaders, and a cruel, heartless death it would be.

"I think you ought to tell the police," advised Frank seriously.

Tom Wat would not hear of this. He shook his head again.

"Chinaboy no tellee police," he declared. "No good. Cause plenty tlouble."

"You seem to be in for plenty of trouble anyway if there's a fellow on your trail with a knife, that's all I can say," remarked Pebbles. "And a dog, too!" he exclaimed as a sudden thought struck him. "I'll bet that animal belonged to Louie Fong. It was *you* the dog was after."

"Mebbe," returned Tom Wat in a subdued, colorless voice.

"Well," said Frank, "we're not going to desert you, that's certain. We'd like to know more about this Louie Fong, too."

Tom Wat's face brightened.

"You help me?"

"Of course we will."

"Personally," observed Sidney Pebbles, "I think you're letting yourself in for a lot of grief. Chinese feuds are good things to leave alone."

# CHAPTER XIV

## THE DISGUISE

LITTLE did the impetuous Hardy boys realize to what lengths they would have to go to fulfill their promise to Tom Wat. They had given their word to help the frightened Chinaman against Louie Fong and his crowd, but as yet they did not realize the extent of their task.

"Where do you live?" said Frank. "Are you still working in Bayport?"

"No workee in Bayport now," returned Tom Wat. "Louie Fong catchee me."

"You can't go back to your old job?"

Tom Wat was firm on this point. Nothing would induce him to return to his old place in the city. If he showed himself at his former haunts, he told them, he would be dead within twenty-four hours.

"Then where do you plan to go?"

The Chinaman said he did not know.

"He had better come with us," Joe suggested. "We can hide him at our house."

"And if Louie Fong catches him there," remarked Sidney Pebbles, "your home will be

turned into a fine imitation of a battlefield.
You'll be dodging flying knives and bullets
from morning until night."

"There's only one answer to that," returned
Joe. "Louie Fong mustn't know he is staying
with us."

"Louie Fong find out some way," muttered
the little Chinaman.

"We'll disguise you," said Frank.

Sidney Pebbles laughed.

"That's an idea. Get him a pair of green
goggles and a long white beard."

Joe regarded the Chinaman solemnly for a
moment.

"Green goggles, nothing," he said suddenly.
"We can dress him up as a girl. He's just
the type."

Tom Wat took alarm at this suggestion. He
shook his head violently.

"No dlessee me up allee samee like girl,"
he objected. "No likee."

"Well, what are you going to do?" asked
Sidney Pebbles. "If you go back to Bayport
as you are now Louie Fong will find you and
that will be your finish."

The Chinaman shivered.

"These boys will take you to their home
and hide you there. You won't have to stay
dressed as a girl all the time. As it is, you
haven't any place to go now."

"No place to go," said Tom Wat sorrow-
fully.

"Will you do it?" asked Frank. "We'll
look after you. There's an extra room at our
house and you'll be quite comfortable."

"Allee light," agreed Tom Wat.

"But where are we going to get clothes for
him if we're going to dress him up as a girl?"
asked Joe.

"That's a problem," Frank admitted.

At this point Sidney Pebbles came to their
assistance.

"We have a few maids working at 'Lantern
Land,'" he said. "They'll be glad to help.
Come to think of it, there is one girl who is
just about Tom Wat's size. Come along and
I'll see what she can do for us."

They left the shelter of the trees, crossed
the road and went into the courtyard. Tom
Wat looked apprehensively from side to side,
evidently afraid that the villainous Louie Fong
might still be hanging about. Sidney Pebbles,
however, set his fears at rest.

"Louie Fong is probably halfway back to
Bayport by now," he said. "He isn't taking
any chances on being caught and arrested for
throwing that knife."

He led them to the side entrance of the roadhouse and they went in. Passing through a
corridor they emerged into a huge main room

with a shimmering dance floor. A pretty girl was dusting furniture.

"Hello, Jean," said Pebbles as the young woman looked up and smiled at them. "How's your wardrobe?"

"My wardrobe?" asked the girl, puzzled. "Why Sidney, you know very well that the wages I get here won't let me dress like the Queen of Sheba."

"Have you an extra outfit you'd like to sell?"

"We'll buy you a new one," volunteered Frank quickly.

"No girl would miss a chance of getting a new outfit," said Jean, dimpling. "What sort of clothes do you want?"

"Just a plain dress, shoes, silk stockings and a hat," said Pebbles. "Our friend here," and he indicated Tom Wat, "has decided that he'd like to dress up as a girl."

Jean looked at the wretched Chinaman and then she began to giggle.

"You aren't joking, are you?"

"Of course we're not joking," returned Sidney Pebbles. "If you have an outfit you'd like to get rid of, hand it over and you'll be saving a human life. This poor chap has an enemy and we want to get him out of here in disguise."

Jean became serious.

"I'll see what I can find in my room."

The girl hurried away.

"No likee," muttered Tom Wat. "No likee dlessee up allee samee girl."

"By the time we get through with you," promised Sidney, "you won't know yourself in the mirror. A little touch of rouge, powder and lipstick and we'll make a new man of you. A new girl, I mean."

Jean returned in a few minutes with the dress and other articles of apparel.

"I think these ought to fit," she said. "He may try them on, anyway."

"Come along, Tom," said Sidney Pebbles "You may use my room for the quick change act."

Reluctantly the Chinaman followed them to a room on the second floor. Sidney tossed the clothes on the bed.

"We'll wait for you."

The boys withdrew, leaving Tom Wat looking dubiously at the garments. They waited in the hall and listened to the subdued grunts and mutterings from beyond the door. The maid, Jean, came upstairs about ten minutes later, just as Tom Wat knocked timidly on the door to signify that he was ready.

"Come on out and let's have a look at you," said Pebbles.

The door opened. A weird object appeared. Tom Wat had done his best but he was quite conscious that his best was not good enough.

The dress, in the first place, was on backwards. He had tried to remedy this defect by hitching up the skirt with a huge safety pin. Modestly he had not removed his trousers and the silk stockings were drawn over the trouser legs in a baggy and shapeless manner. He tottered on the high heels of the shoes and the hat was awry.

"No likee," he muttered.

The girl burst into a shriek of laughter. A moment later she was joined by Sidney Pebbles and the Hardy boys. They roared with mirth. Tom Wat glared at them.

"No jokee!" he said.

"Oh, it's too funny!" gasped the girl. "He has *everything* on wrong."

An elderly, near-sighted chambermaid came down the hall at that moment. Curiously she advanced toward them, took one look at Tom Wat, stared and said:

"Mercy! It's a female tramp! Mr. Pebbles, get that woman out of this place at once."

Sidney Pebbles controlled his mirth.

"Go back in there and try again," he said to Tom Wat. "You don't wear silk stockings over your trousers. Take the pants off. And you have the dress on backward."

The chambermaid shrieked and fled. Jean became hysterical. Tom Wat, grumbling, went back into the room and slammed the door.

"I'll go and lend him a hand," said Frank.

A little later, when he emerged with Tom Wat again, the disguise was more than passable. The dress fitted his slight figure perfectly, the hat drooped coyly over one eye and the stockings were trim and neat. Jean clapped her hands.

"Why, that's simply perfect!" she exclaimed. "Now a little touch of make-up——"

She fled toward her own room and returned quickly with powder, rouge and lipstick. She advanced upon the embarrassed Tom Wat.

"No likee. No likee," he said hastily, backing away.

Frank and Joe snickered.

"Whether you like it or not you're going to be disguised properly," said the girl firmly as she grasped his chin. "Hold still, now."

Expertly she dabbed rouge and powder on his cheeks, applied lipstick, pencilled his eyebrows and then stood back to survey her handiwork.

"There!" she announced proudly. "What do you think of him now?"

"He's a knockout!" exclaimed Sidney Pebbles jubilantly.

And to tell the truth, it would have taken more than a second glance to penetrate Tom Wat's disguise. He stood before them as a neat, shy and rather pretty girl, his delicate features and clear complexion adding to the effect. Jean was enthusiastic.

"He could go on the stage. That make-up would fool anyone," she said.

"It should fool Louie Fong, at any rate," remarked Joe. "Now let's get back to Bayport."

In the face of all this approval Tom Wat lost some of his resentment against his changed appearance. He went back into the room, regarded himself critically in the mirror, and then smiled.

"How I walk?" he inquired in a high voice. "Likee this?" And he tripped daintily across the room in an excellent imitation of a girlish walk.

"You'll do," grinned Pebbles. "You'll get away with it as long as you don't talk too much. And you mustn't forget to giggle every few minutes, for no reason at all, and powder your nose whenever you see a mirror."

The boys thanked Jean for her assistance and promised to replace the borrowed clothing with a new outfit as soon as they could make the necessary purchases in Bayport.

"On one condition," Sidney Pebbles reminded her.

"What is that?" she inquired.

"You're to forget all about this. You don't remember that a Chinaman ever came in here this morning or that you ever helped dress him up as a girl.''

"I won't breathe a word of it," she promised.

"Good.''

They went downstairs and left the roadhouse. Out in the courtyard Sidney Pebbles gave Tom Wat a final inspection and declared that he would pass for a girl in any company.

"You chaps had better keep in touch with me," he said to the Hardy boys. "If I can help you at all I'll be glad to do so. And besides, I'm curious to know more about this chap who is using my name.''

"And your face," laughed Joe.

"The face is probably his own but it's dollars to doughnuts that the name isn't. If he is going around robbing people's houses I'll find myself in jail by mistake if he isn't stopped.''

"We'll let you know if we hear anything more about him," said Frank.

They said goodbye to their new friend and went down the road with Tom Wat, who did not appear at all cheerful in his unaccustomed garb. By the time they reached the roadster, however, the boys had persuaded him that it was far better to endure a little inconvenience and remain alive than to court death at the hands of Louie Fong and his gang.

# CHAPTER XV

### THE SECRET GUEST

"I'm jealous," said Callie Shaw.

"So am I," added Iola Morton.

"And I," remarked Chet Morton, "am going to take you two lads to task for holding out on me."

Frank and Joe tried to look innocent. It was early that afternoon, after Tom Wat had been quietly smuggled into the Hardy home and they were driving down High Street, when their friends called to them from the sidewalk.

Callie Shaw, a pretty, brown-eyed girl whom Frank particularly admired was a close friend of Iola Morton, Chet's sister. Although Joe Hardy was never known to pay any special attention to girls it was well known that he was willing to concede that Iola was "all right —as a girl." This, from Joe, almost amounted to flattery.

"Do you understand?" laughed Callie, looking at Frank. "I repeat that I'm jealous."

"Me too," declared Iola, looking at Joe.

"You're both in wrong," chuckled Chet

114

"Come on. Tell us all about it. Who is the new girl friend and whose particular girl friend is she?"

"What girl friend?" asked Frank.

"No use pretending you don't know what we're talking about. The girls know all about it so you may as well 'fess up. Who was the swell-looking girl you two were driving with this morning?"

"Who said we were driving with a swell-looking girl?" asked Joe.

"I said so," returned Chet. "And I repeat it. As a matter of fact, I saw you. I nearly tumbled off my motorcycle. Who is she, anyway? Couldn't you give a fellow an introduction? New girl in town?"

"Sorry," said Frank airily, "but she's very particular about the company she keeps."

"Oh!" exclaimed Chet. "She's very particular about the company she keeps, eh? Well, well! What does she mean by going driving with you two, then?"

"That's right, Chet," laughed Iola. "Don't let them bluff you."

"Well—as a matter of fact," explained Joe, "she was with us—sort of by accident."

"It didn't look much like an accident to me," said Chet. "There she was, sitting right between the pair of you, as if she'd known you for years."

"What's her name, Frank?" asked Callie.

"I—I don't know," stuttered Frank. He could not very well explain that the mysterious friend's name was Tom Wat. And neither of the boys had thought of a suitable girl's name for their disguised guest.

"You don't know!" scoffed Chet. "Tell that to the marines. Why, you took her right into your house. Who is she, Joe?"

Joe racked his brains for a suitable name to bestow on Tom Wat but he could think of nothing.

"What's her name, Joe?" urged Iola.

"Wat," blurted Joe.

"I said 'What's her name?' " repeated Iola.

"And I said 'Wat,' " replied Joe.

"I know you did. Couldn't you hear me? What's her name?"

"Her name," said Joe desperately, "is Wat. Miss Wat."

"Oh, I see. Miss Wat?"

"Miss what?" demanded Chet.

"Yes," said Joe.

Chet frowned. "Which one of us is crazy now?" he inquired. "I said, 'Miss what?' "

"And I said 'yes,' " shouted Joe.

"That's no answer to a civil question," Chet growled.

"The girl's name," Iola informed him sweetly, "is Miss Wat."

"Oh!" said Chet. "Now we know what's what."

"Anything else?" inquired Frank.

"Say, look here," objected Chet, "it seems to me that you two are holding out a secret on us. I'd like to know more about this mysterious Miss Wat."

"So say we all," added Callie Shaw.

"We'll be late for our engagement," observed Joe, for he saw that this argument might lead to complications. "Sorry. Afraid we must be going."

"Sorry!" chanted Frank, and the roadster lurched away.

Chet glared after them.

"We didn't get much satisfaction, did we?" laughed Callie. "They don't seem inclined to talk about their new friend."

"I scent a mystery here," said Chet. "And when Chet Morton scents a mystery he doesn't rest until he has solved it."

The Hardy boys were not wholly at ease as they drove away from their friends. They realized, however, that if they had stayed they might have let slip some vital information. They knew Chet's remorseless method of questioning. So far their secret had been well kept.

Neither Nurse Cody nor Aunt Gertrude knew of the presence of the Chinaman on the third floor of the Hardy home. Aunt Gertrude would have certainly suffered a relapse had she known of the extra guest. Tom Wat had been hidden in the drawing-room while Joe had lured Nurse Cody to the kitchen on the pretext of making up a grocery order. Frank had then hustled the frightened Tom Wat up the stairs. Aunt Gertrude was asleep at the time. Safe in his third-floor room Tom Wat had been provided with a few sandwiches and told to make himself comfortable.

The boys were now on their way to seek another interview with Orrin North in Lakeside. They were in hopes that the ship owner might tell them something of the case on which Fenton Hardy had been working.

"If he would only tell us," said Frank, "we might be able to do something. Things may be in a terrible mess by the time Dad gets back."

"I think they're in a bad mess right now," said Joe. "Somehow, I have a feeling that Louie Fong is at the bottom of the whole business."

When they reached Lakeside they drove at once to Orrin North's office. When they inquired for the ship owner, however, the clerk in the outer room shook his head.

"He's away for the afternoon. You won't be able to see him until tomorrow morning."

The boys were disappointed.

"Did he leave town?" asked Frank.

"Oh, no. He went to the ball game."

"Then we might be able to find him there."

"Stranger things have happened," replied the clerk, with the air of one who has just said something very smart.

They drove out to the ball park. The game had already started for they could hear a roar of cheers from beyond the high board fence that encircled the grounds.

"Shall we go in?" asked Frank as he brought the car to a stop.

"We'll have a hard time finding him in that crowd," said Joe. "Perhaps we'd better wait until the game is over."

"That won't be for a couple of hours. If Mr. North is a baseball fan perhaps he has a season ticket. I'll ask one of the gatemen."

The Lakeside ball park was not very large and the town was not a very big one. It was more than probable, reflected Frank, that the gateman would know exactly where Orrin North was sitting. He got out of the car and went over to the entrance.

"Is Mr. North at the game?" he inquired.

"Whenever there is a game," returned the attendant, "you can be sure Orrin North is here. Yes, he just came in a few minutes ago."

"Does he always take the same seat?"

The man shook his head.

"No reserved seats in this place, sonny," he replied. "But I can tell you where Mr. North can be found. He's right in the top row at the south side of the field. If you walk along outside the fence you'll be able to see him. Better buy a ticket and come in."

"I'll see what my brother thinks about it."

Frank returned to the car and told Joe what the gateman had said.

"No need of going in if we can see him from outside the fence. We'll save a dollar. We can call to him and maybe he'll come out for a few minutes."

They got out of their automobile and walked along beneath the board fence toward the south side of the ball park. They could plainly see the heads and shoulders of spectators above the top of the fence.

"If he is in the top row of seats we can't miss him," said Frank.

They reached the south side of the park and as they walked along they carefully scanned the row of backs above them. Every once in a while they could hear the crack of ball against bat, and the roar of cheers that punctuate the progress of every game.

"There he is," said Joe suddenly. "Just ahead of us. In the gray suit and straw hat."

There was no mistaking the heavy shoulders and bullet-like head of Orrin North. He was chewing at a cigar. Beside him sat a man in a cap and a loud check suit. The pair were in earnest conversation and were apparently paying no attention to the ball game.

Standing at the bottom of the fence, a few feet below Orrin North and his friend, the boys were undecided as to their next move. They did not care to interrupt the ship owner's conversation.

"Better wait until they've finished their chat," Frank suggested. "Then we'll shout up to him."

It was soon obvious that the conversation between North and his friend was no casual affair. Then one word, spoken by the stranger in a tone that carried clearly to the boys beneath the fence, electrified the young listeners.

The word was "Hardy."

Frank and Joe were surprised. This conversation, then, had something to do with them or with their father. So far they had made no effort to overhear what North and his friend were saying. Now they were interested. Presently the ship owner remarked in a harsh voice:

"Hardy? Why bother about him? He's no good. He is out of town."

The other man said something which the boys could not catch.

"Good detective?" snapped North impatiently. "I don't believe it. Why, even those

Chinese robbed his place. Why pay him for his work?"

Orrin North evidently realized just then that he had been speaking too loudly for he lowered his voice and the pair resumed their conversation in tones that were inaudible to the Hardy boys. After a while they turned their attention to the ball game.

By common consent Frank and Joe withdrew. "I don't think we'd better talk to Mr. North today," decided Frank.

"Not until we learn more about him," agreed Joe. "I never did trust that fellow, anyway."

# CHAPTER XVI

## THE STRANGE SPY

MORE than ever now the Hardy boys were convinced that they must take the lead if they were to protect their father's interests. The fragment of conversation they had overheard at the ball park had not tended to increase their confidence in Orrin North. When they returned home that afternoon they went eagerly to the mail-box in the hope that a letter might have arrived from their parents. But they were disappointed.

"We'll just have to carry on until he comes back," said Frank. "We're working in the dark, worse luck."

"I think we were wise in leaving the ball park. If North knew we were out there this afternoon he might suspect that we had overheard him."

"We're on our guard against him now. I think it would be a good idea to see him, just the same, as we had planned."

"We might get some information," agreed Joe. "What do you say we go out tonight?"

123

"All right with me. Let's go up first and see how Tom Wat is getting along. He must be lonesome."

They went upstairs. In the hallway they met Nurse Cody.

"How is Aunt Gertrude?" they inquired.

"Not much better but she's certainly no worse," said Mrs. Cody. "Rest and quiet is all she needs. Her nerves are all upset, poor thing. And I'm not surprised. I'm beginning to wonder if my own nerves are all that they should be."

"Why is that?" asked Frank.

Nurse Cody frowned and pointed to the ceiling.

"Noises!"

"Why—what sort of noises?" said Joe.

"Queer noises. Just as if someone was prowling around up there."

"How could there be anyone upstairs?" laughed Frank, ill at ease lest Nurse Cody should take it into her head to investigate. "Did you go up and look around?"

"Not me!" replied the nurse promptly. "My job is to attend to my patient. But I'm sure I've heard noises up there this afternoon. Not a sound did I hear all morning but this afternoon I've had a queer feelin' that there's somebody up there."

"In that case," said Joe, "we'll go up ourselves. If there's a burglar in the house we'll rout him out."

"Now do be careful!" she urged nervously.

"Don't worry," they assured her. "We'll look after ourselves."

They went on up to the third floor. In his room they found Tom Wat lying on his bed, fast asleep. He had taken off the girl's clothes and was now in his ordinary attire. He awakened when they entered the room.

"Whatamalla?" he whispered.

"Everything is fine," replied Frank quietly. "How are you getting along?"

"Good. Velly quiet."

"Better be careful when you're walking around up here. The nurse heard you. Take your shoes off and walk in your sock feet. Hungry?"

"Not yet."

"We'll smuggle some food up at supper time."

"You see Louie Fong?" asked the Chinaman anxiously.

"No, we haven't seen him. Don't worry about Louie Fong. You're quite safe here."

They went downstairs again.

"No burglars up there," they assured Mrs. Cody truthfully. "You can set your mind at rest."

"Well, I'm glad to hear it," replied the good

woman. "It must have been my imagination but I was sure I heard somebody movin' about. You couldn't get me to go up there for a million dollars."

The boys were glad to hear that, although they did not say so. It meant that Tom Wat was safe from discovery.

That evening they were permitted to see Aunt Gertrude for a few minutes. She still looked pale and tired but she had rested well during the day and the lads were satisfied that it was only a matter of time before she would be up and about once more.

"I'm sure it's very good of you to get a nurse to look after your old aunt," she told them gratefully. "You're good boys, in spite of all the scoldings that I've given you. Well," she amended with a faint smile, "maybe you're good *because* of the scoldings."

"I guess we deserved them, Aunt Gertrude," said Frank with a smile. "If there's anything more we can do to make you comfortable, be sure to let us know."

"I'm being well looked after. Now, lads, run along and play."

Aunt Gertrude could never rid herself of an idea that her nephews were about six and seven years of age respectively.

When they left their relative they were at a loss as to what to do next. They chafed at any delay in reaching the solution of the strange mystery in which they had become involved, and yet every move they made seemed to entangle matters more than ever. Joe was firmly of the opinion that they should still seek their interview with Orrin North.

"He doesn't know we suspect him," Joe pointed out. "If he is working against Dad we ought to keep an eye on the situation."

"The trouble is," remarked Frank, "that we don't know the situation."

"It would certainly help if we knew why North employed Dad. After all, he might tell us. It will do no harm to ask. Let's go to Lakeside tonight and have a talk with him."

"I'm game. And let's take Tom Wat with us. The fresh air will do him good."

Nurse Cody went to bed early that evening, so the coast was clear. At about nine o'clock the boys went quietly upstairs, told Tom Wat that they were going to take him for a drive, and brought the young Chinaman down to the lower part of the house. It was after dark so they did not think it necessary for him to resume his disguise.

"Where you go?" asked Tom, when they went out to the garage and took their places in the roadster.

"We're going out to Lakeside to see Orrin North," Frank explained. "You won't have to get out of the car. No one will notice you."

Tom Wat frowned.

"Ollin No'th bad fella!" he said. "Me no likee."

"Why don't you like him?" asked Joe, hoping that Tom Wat might be able to throw some light on the ship owner's real character.

"No talkee," grunted Tom in his secretive manner. "No likee."

They could get no more out of him. He was not disposed to discuss the reasons for his dislike of Orrin North, but it was quite plain to the Hardy boys that he hated the man intensely.

Frank wondered why Tom Wat should have any reason for disliking North. Was it possible that the man had dealings with the Chinese of Bayport?

Reaching Lakeside, they drove toward Mr. North's office. The place was in darkness, but as they approached the driveway leading to a garage at the rear of the building a big touring car sped silently past the roadster.

Tom Wat leaned forward as the car went by. He uttered a little gasp and sank back, drawing his hat down over his face.

"What's the matter?" asked Frank.

For a moment the Chinaman did not answer. Then he whispered in a voice vibrant with fear:

"Louie Fong."

"Louie Fong!" exclaimed Joe. "You couldn't see him."

"Louie Fong car."

Frank whistled. Louie Fong driving to the garage back of North's office late at night? This was more than suspicious. He drove on past the driveway and parked the roadster half way down the block.

"I think we'll look into this," he said quietly to his brother.

"Me no go," muttered Tom Wat.

"You stay here," they told him. "We won't be long."

They went back up the street and slipped quietly into the shadows of the driveway. They could see the red tail-light of the car in the yard. There was a light in a rear window of North's office building. A moment later this light went out.

The Hardy boys crouched close beside the fence and watched. They heard footsteps crunching on the gravel and caught a glimpse of a dim figure pacing up and down near the garage. A moment later they heard a brusque, familiar voice.

"That you, Louie?"

The answer was inaudible, but they could hear a key grate in a lock, the screech of hinges as the garage door was opened. A light shone from the garage window. Through the glass they had a momentary glimpse of the evil, yellow face of Louie Fong. Then it vanished. They saw the red, square visage of Orrin North, who came over toward the window. A shade was pulled down.

Joe would have moved forward but Frank gripped his arm.

"Not yet," he whispered.

What business could have brought Orrin North and Louie Fong together for this secret and private night conference?

A moment later they were thankful that they had not moved out of their hiding place by the fence. They heard the quiet hum of an engine, then the faint slither of tires upon the pavement. A car, running without lights, slid up to the entrance of the driveway. It was like a phantom. Silently it came to a stop. A man stepped out, and the car was driven on past the gateway.

The newcomer moved quietly into the yard. He wore a long coat, the collar of which was turned up so as to conceal his features. His face was further hidden by the brim of a slouch hat drawn low upon his forehead.

Frank and Joe were breathless with excitement. Had they been seen? Was this a third member of the meeting? Had he spied them hiding by the fence?

The stranger came directly toward them.

For a moment they were positive that he must have seen them. But he passed by, head down, hands thrust into his coat pockets.

He did not go toward the door of the garage. Instead, he went to the back of Louie Fong's car. Here he knelt down and examined the number plate. Then, evidently satisfied, he strode off into the shadows.

The man was lost to sight but the boys could hear his footsteps as he cautiously crept along the side of the garage. Then they saw his shadow against the wall. He was crouching beneath the window.

"He didn't come here to meet them at all," whispered Joe.

"Shh! He's a spy."

Their own hopes of overhearing the interview between Louie Fong and Orrin North were destroyed. This unknown eavesdropper's appearance on the scene had complicated the mystery. Was he friend or foe? Chinaman or white man?

They crouched where they were and waited. The yard was in silence. Dimly they could see that dark, sinister figure beneath the window.

Then suddenly the garage door was flung open. A beam of brilliant light fell across the yard. Louie Fong stood on the threshold, peering out into the night!

# CHAPTER XVII

## ORRIN NORTH EXPLAINS

So abrupt, so unexpected was the appearance of the Chinaman that the Hardy boys were taken completely by surprise. They dared not move, yet they were sure they had been seen.

Either that, or the mysterious stranger had made some noise that had attracted Louie Fong's attention. The Chinaman stood on the threshold looking out into the night. Frank and Joe waited in an agony of suspense.

The stranger, whoever he was, kept cool. He did not reveal his presence by a sound. He flattened himself against the side of the garage and remained as motionless as a statue.

Presently Orrin North appeared in the doorway behind the Chinaman. The two talked in low tones for a moment as they came out of the building. North reached inside the door and switched out the light. As the door slammed, a lock clicked.

"All right then," Orrin North said clearly, "I'll see you tomorrow."

North went back toward his office, while Louie Fong came directly across the yard toward his car. His shoes made no sound; he was as quiet and sinister as a cat.

Even yet the Hardy boys were uneasy. They were not convinced that the Chinaman had not seen them. They knew he was sly and quick and that even now his keen eyes might be watching them as they crouched in the shadow beneath the fence.

However, Louie Fong went directly to his automobile and stepped inside. The engine throbbed. The car backed slowly out into the main road.

Frank gripped Joe by the wrist and pointed toward the garage. The shadowy figure by the wall was melting into the gloom. The stranger vanished without a sound.

They waited until they heard Louie Fong's car speeding away, then they slipped out of the courtyard and ran back to their own roadster. There was no sign of the car that had brought the mysterious stranger to the scene. Frank wrenched open the door of the roadster. Then he gasped.

"Where's Tom Wat?"

The roadster was deserted. Tom Wat had disappeared. Joe uttered an exclamation of dismay.

"Maybe Louie Fong found him!"

There was a sudden rustling among the bushes at the roadside. A figure emerged from the ditch. To their relief they saw it was none other than Tom Wat.

"Me hide," he explained laconically.

"Boy, you gave us a scare," said Joe. "We thought he had kidnaped you."

They scrambled into the car and drove down the road about half a mile. Then Frank brought the roadster to a stop.

"What next?" he said.

"What's your suggestion? Back to Bayport?"

"We haven't accomplished much yet."

"I think we've learned plenty," said Joe. "We know that Orrin North and Louie Fong have some business that brings them together secretly at night. And we know that someone else is interested enough to spy on them."

"Yes, we found out that," Frank agreed, "but are we any better off? The whole business is more mysterious than ever."

"That's true enough."

"We came out here to speak to Orrin North. As far as I can see there's no reason why we shouldn't go ahead with our program."

"I wish," muttered Joe, "I knew what he and Louie Fong were talking about. Tom, did you ever hear that North and Louie Fong were mixed up in any business affairs?"

Tom Wat could not enlighten them. The boys thought that the little man had his own suspicions as to the nature of the dealings between the pair but that he was afraid to voice them. Tom Wat's obvious terror of Louie Fong impressed them with the fact that in the sinister Chinaman they were dealing with a dangerous and powerful antagonist.

"Let's drive back to the office," suggested Frank. "He won't know we've already been near the place."

"All right!"

Frank turned the car about and they drove back. But the office was in darkness. They were too late. Orrin North had departed.

"Gone home for the night," said Joe.

"There's no law against going to his house, wherever that is. We'll go downtown and ask someone to tell us the way."

An obliging constable on Lakeside's main street told them that Orrin North lived out in the country.

"He has a homestead about two miles out of town," said the officer. "As a matter of fact, I think he's just gone out there. His car passed this way a few minutes ago."

Orrin North's idea of "homesteading" was evidently very modern. His huge stone residence was really a luxurious country home and the driveway leading from the main road was flanked by trim hedges and well-kept grounds.

"There must be money in the shipping business," commented Frank as they drove up to the house.

They left Tom Wat in the car and went up to the door. A maid answered the bell.

"Mr. North just came in," she told the boys. "What names shall I give?"

They told her and she went away, returning a few minutes later to say that Mr. North would see them. The girl ushered them into a comfortable library. The books were arranged so neatly upon the shelves, however, that the boys doubted if Orrin North ever bothered to read any of them. He was smoking as he read his newspaper. The man looked up, scowling.

"Can't spare you much time," North growled. "Just got in after a hard day's work. What is it now?"

"We haven't been able to locate Dad yet," Frank informed him.

"Blast the luck! I don't see how any man can go away and leave his business in such shape that no one knows what's what. I know I couldn't afford to do it. Well, if you can't get in touch with him, there's only one thing for me to do. I'll have to get someone else to handle the business for me."

"We have taken care of some of Dad's cases

for him at other times when he has been away,"
ventured Joe.

Orrin North laughed shortly.

"Must have been mighty small ones," he
grunted.

"We were thinking," said Frank, "that if
you would tell us just which case Dad was
working on, we might be able to help you."

"Listen!" said North scornfully. "When I
asked your pa to take hold of this matter I was
hirin' an expert detective, see? Not a couple
of kids. You don't think I'm goin' to pay him
to work for me and have him turn the business
over to his youngsters, do you?"

"We're not saying we can do as well as Dad
or anywhere nearly as well," returned Frank
with spirit. "But we're not amateurs entirely.
He has taught us a good deal. At least we can
look after his interests until he returns."

"Nope!" snapped North. "If your pa
doesn't come back in a day or so I'm going to
hire me another detective. This case is too big
for kids."

"Why not tell us what it's all about? We
may be able to suggest something."

"Oh, so far as that goes, I don't mind telling
you what it's about. But you won't be able to
help me any, I promise you that."

"We can try," said Joe.

"The situation is this," said North. "I've

got enemies who are tryin' to ruin my reputation."

"How?"

"By accusin' me of smuggling, blast it!" he roared, pounding the table with his fist. "Me! Me that's never had a black mark against my name since I went into the shipping business. That's what it's about."

"What sort of smuggling?" asked Frank.

Orrin North leaned forward.

"Chinamen!" he rasped.

"You're accused of smuggling Chinamen!"

"That's right. You know there's a heavy head tax on every Chinaman that comes into the country. There's good money to be made by any man who can smuggle 'em in. And that's what they're sayin' about me. They say I'm doin' a regular business of it."

"Who accuses you?" asked Frank.

"Plenty of people," returned the ship owner vaguely. "There's been hints gone in to the Department of Immigration. There was an inspector here just the other day askin' me questions. Smugglin' Chinamen!" he snorted. "Furthest thing from my mind. I'm an honest man. I make enough money in honest trade without turning crooked. I don't have to go into that game to make money."

"But no definite charge has ever been laid against you," Frank pointed out.

"Of course not. And why? Because they haven't got any evidence against me, that's why. And they never will have. But these rumors are enough to blacken my good name. They hurt my reputation in shippin' circles. Within the past couple of weeks I've lost two good customers. Don't care to give their trade to a man suspected of smugglin', they said."

"Who is behind the rumors?" asked Joe.

"I wish I knew," fumed Orrin North. "I've got my suspicions. I've got rivals in the shipping business who would be glad to steal trade away from me if they could. And they're doing it, all on account of these smugglin' stories."

"And what did you want Dad to do for you?"

"Why, to protect my interests, of course!" exclaimed Orrin North. "I employed him in self-defence. If these enemies of mine are trying to get the authorities after me and ruin me, why I've just got to fight fire with fire. I said I'd hire the best detective I could get. Chinamen *are* bein' smuggled in along this coast. I know that. We all know it. If your pa could find out who is really doin' the smugglin' it would clear my reputation. That's why I hired him."

"Had he done any work on the case before he went away?" Joe asked.

"How do I know?" demanded North.

"Matter of fact, I don't think he did a tap of work on it. Never told me a thing. I tell you I'm mighty tired of the way he acted in this business. If these rumors keep up I'll find myself forced into a big court case to protect myself and it'll cost me a fortune."

He got up from his chair and stamped up and down the room.

"I'll be ruined if I don't put a stop to them stories," he raged, "and the only way to stop 'em is to find out who *is* doing this smugglin'. Now," he said, grinning scornfully at the boys, "do you think you can take up a job that your pa has run away from? Matter of fact, I think he found it was too big for him and just went away so he wouldn't have to admit he was licked."

Frank bit his lip. He did not care to hear these reflections on his father's ability, but he knew he must control his temper.

"I don't think Dad ran away from the case," said Frank. "In fact, I'm sure he didn't. There is some other explanation. If you'll let my brother and me look after things until he comes back you won't have any cause to regret it."

"No! No!" declared North. "This isn't a case for youngsters. If it's too big for your pa it's miles too big for you. Run along home, now. It's late and I want to go to bed."

Thus dismissed, the Hardy boys left the brusque mannered ship owner. They were crestfallen at the curt reception their offer of help had been accorded. Nevertheless, they had made some progress.

"We got what we came after," Frank reminded his brother. "We know the case Dad was working on, at any rate."

"And somehow," muttered Joe, "I don't like the looks of that case. What do you think of it yourself?"

"It strikes me," replied Frank seriously, "that Orrin North isn't quite as honest as he pretends to be."

"Where there is smoke there is fire."

"If people accuse him of smuggling Chinamen into the country they must have some grounds for the rumors. Of course, it may be as he claims. He may have enemies who are trying to ruin him."

"I don't trust him," declared Joe firmly.

"I wish Dad would come back. We could talk things over with him."

They found Tom Wat waiting for them in the car, but on the way home told him nothing about their interview with Orrin North. As they came within sight of their house on High Street Joe suddenly slapped his knee and exclaimed:

"I have an idea!"

# CHAPTER XVIII

### BACK TO THE LAUNDRY

Joe's idea was simple. It was, in fact, that they return to the garage back of Orrin North's office the next day to see if they could find some clue to the identity of the mysterious stranger.

"The ground in that yard was soft," Joe pointed out. "We may be able to find his footprints."

"What if Mr. North sees us hanging around his garage?" Frank objected.

"He won't find us. Not if we go early enough."

"There may be some truth in that story about smuggled Chinamen. The fact that North is mixed up with Louie Fong is suspicious."

"Perhaps that stranger was one of Mr. North's enemies," suggested Joe.

"Trying to get evidence against him. It's not unlikely. In any case, your idea is worth following up. I'd like to know who that stranger was."

They decided to set the alarm for four o'clock, since they were eager to make their investigations at the North garage at a time when they would not be disturbed. At that early hour none of the office employees would be on the scene and it was highly improbable that the boys would be noticed by anyone.

Tom Wat returned to his room on the third floor of the house. He came in unobserved, for Nurse Cody and Aunt Gertrude were asleep.

Promptly at four o'clock the shattering clamor of the alarm clock awakened the boys. It was summer time and dawn came early so there was plenty of light for their morning journey.

"Can't wait for breakfast," decided Frank as they hurriedly dressed. "We'll make a quick run out to Lakeside, look around and then hurry back."

"I'll bring along a tape measure. If we find any footprints we'd better keep a record of them."

They went quietly down the stairs. In the second floor hall they listened for a moment at the door of Aunt Gertrude's room. They heard only the regular, muffled snores of the nurse.

"We'll be back before they know we've gone," whispered Frank.

They slipped out of the house and crossed

the dew-drenched grass in the clear, crisp air of morning.

"All clear so far," laughed Joe, as they scrambled into the car. In a few minutes they were speeding swiftly out of Bayport.

They met only a few milk wagons and market trucks on the road at that hour and when they reached Lakeside they found the street near the North office deserted, as they had expected. They parked the car and made their way quickly into the yard where they had hidden the previous night.

They wasted no time in exploring the place, but made their way at once toward the garage. The ground, as Joe had recalled, was soft. Frank stooped down, examining the soil at the place where the mysterious stranger had crouched beneath the window.

"What more could we want?" he exclaimed softly.

He pointed to the earth at his feet. There, clear and distinct, was the print of a man's shoe. Further on, along the side of the garage, they found other similar footmarks.

Joe whipped out the tape measure. Swiftly he took measurements and jotted down the figures on the back of an envelope. On a sheet of paper he drew a rough diagram of the mark. Frank, in the meantime, made an investigation of the ground nearby on the chance that the

stranger might have dropped something that
would afford a more tangible clue.

"Just the footprints," he reported when he
came back a moment later.

"Better than nothing," commented Joe.
"Let's get out of here before someone sees us."

They hastened away and within a few minutes were speeding back to Bayport. It was
not quite five o'clock when they were safely
back in their own room, the car was back in
the garage and not another soul had been the
wiser about their adventure.

"I have a hunch about these footprints,"
said Joe, opening the drawer of the writing
desk in their room. "They seem familiar,
somehow." He took out the sheets upon which
had been recorded the tracings and measurements of the footprints they had found under
the window on the morning after the disappearance of Sidney Pebbles. "We'll just check up
on these."

The boys bent over the desk as Joe laid the
papers side by side. They consulted the figures. Suddenly Frank slapped his brother on
the back.

"Why—they're the same!" he exclaimed.

"Exactly the same."

"Then the man who left the footprints under
the window was the same man who spied on
Orrin North and Louie Fong last night!"

"According to the footprints. Of course, we can't be sure. But the evidence is fairly clear."

"I should say it is," declared Frank.

"Sidney Pebbles, the First?"

"Or the Chinaman who might have come into the house when Aunt Gertrude was lying on the couch. Maybe he wasn't a dream."

Their discovery was important. Yet it was very tantalizing. If they could only learn the identity of the stranger who had crouched beside North's garage they would probably know the identity of the stranger who had left the footprints under the window. That knowledge would go a long way toward clearing up the mystery. But they seemed as far away from solving the problem as when they had started.

"We'll just have to keep plugging away," declared Frank. "In all the other mysteries we tackled we had plenty of setbacks. Then something usually happened to straighten everything out, and all the points that had puzzled us became as clear as day."

"What's the next stop, then?"

"Louie Fong's laundry."

Joe was thoughtful.

"I don't think we'll get much information there. Louie Fong is too careful."

"We'll take Tom Wat with us. In disguise. If he hears any Chinese talk he'll be able to interpret it. We have to go there for the laundry in any case.  After breakfast we'll drop in at Louie Fong's place."

"I'll bet Tom Wat will just about cheer out loud when he hears that," grinned Joe.  "He isn't any more afraid of Louie Fong than he is of a rattlesnake."

After a while the boys heard Nurse Cody moving about downstairs so they went to the kitchen, trying to look like lads who had just awakened after a long night's sleep.

"How are you this morning, Mrs. Cody?" they greeted her.

Mrs. Cody looked up from the stove.

"Tolerable," she said.  "Just tolerable.  Of course, when a body doesn't get her rightful sleep it's not to be expected that she'll go hopping and skipping about and whistlin' like a bird in the morning."

"Didn't you sleep well?" asked Frank.  He wondered if their early morning departure had awakened the nurse.

"Not a wink did I sleep the livelong night," she assured them mournfully.  "That is, not more than to doze off for a few minutes now and then."

The boys, remembering the snores they had heard from beyond the bedroom door, were of the private opinion that Nurse Cody had slept much better than she imagined.

"And when I *did* sleep," she continued, "I

dreamed. I dreamed continual. About cats."

"You dreamed about cats?" said Joe.

"Cats. And it's a bad sign. It means that there's trouble hangin' over the house. I never knew it to fail. Last time I dreamed about cats, do you know what happened? My cousin's brother-in-law, out in Seattle, fell off the back porch and broke his leg. That's what it means to dream about cats."

She shook her head solemnly.

"How is Aunt Gertrude this morning?" inquired Frank.

"She had a good night. Her nerves are in bad shape yet, though. She was asking about you lads. Better go up and see her."

The boys went upstairs and found their aunt awake and muttering to herself as she tossed restlessly on the bed.

"Hello, Aunt Gertrude!" exclaimed Frank cheerfully. "You look as fit as a fiddle this morning. Do you think you'll be getting up today?"

"I'm *not* as fit as a fiddle!" snapped the patient. "And if I'm up within the month I'll be lucky. This place will go to rack and ruin now that I'm laid up, I suppose."

This was more like the old Aunt Gertrude. That she could summon sufficient strength to be irritable was a sure sign that she was recovering rapidly.

"Straighten your necktie, boy!" she barked at Joe. "Unless I'm here to look after you I'll warrant you go around looking like a savage. And you, Frank—when did you shine your shoes last?"

Frank looked guiltily at the offending footwear. Traces of the muddy clay from the yard back of North's office were plainly visible on his shoes.

"Why—yesterday," he said meekly.

"I don't believe it. You get busy with the brush and blacking, young man, or I'll make it hot for you. Oh dear, oh dear! If I could only get better. My poor nerves!"

"Didn't you sleep well?" asked Joe.

"As well as might be expected," she snapped. "Which means I didn't sleep a wink."

"Mrs. Cody said she didn't sleep a wink, either," observed Frank. "You must have had a long night's talk."

"None of your impudence! How can a person sleep when she sees a Chinaman every time she closes her eyes? How can she? I can't get that terrible dream out of my mind."

"You mean the one about the man with the knife?" asked Joe.

"Now what other dream *could* I mean? At that, I'm not sure if it was a dream or not. It was so vivid that it might be true. I can't get that man's terrible face out of my mind for a minute. I keep thinking there's a Chinaman right in this house."

The boys thought of Tom Wat in the upstairs room.

"You boys have been up to something!" said Aunt Gertrude sharply. "Don't tell me you haven't. I can tell by your faces. What is it? What mischief have you been up to now?"

"None at all," said Frank.

"Hmmph! You *would* say that, of course. Well, I'll hear all about it as soon as I'm well again, never fear. Run along now."

"Aunty," said Joe, "can you remember the young fellow who got you the drink of water on the boat? Can you recall what he looked like?"

"Sidney Pebbles," prompted Frank.

"Sidney Pebbles?" retorted Aunt Gertrude. "Who's he? I don't know any Pebbles." She laughed shortly. "He isn't the only pebble on the beach. Ha! Ha!"

Aunt Gertrude seemed to think she had achieved an excellent joke and laughed so heartily that she was almost in a good humor.

"No," she told them, "I can't remember any of the people on the boat. The whole trip seems like a trance. I can't recall what anyone looked like. It gives me a headache to try to think."

Pettishly, she dismissed them, so the boys went downstairs and had breakfast. Mrs. Cody edified them by reading her teacup, in which she saw a great variety of interesting events, which included a journey across water, a meeting with a dark man, a procession—whether wedding or funeral she wasn't sure—an accident, several dozen letters and a warning against going for airplane flights. Afterward, when she had brought breakfast to Aunt Gertrude and was relating all these wonders out of the one teacup, the boys slipped upstairs to Tom Wat's room.

"Quick!" urged Frank. "Hop into the girl's clothes. We're going to call on a friend of yours."

Tom regarded the disguise without enthusiasm.

"Where we go?" he asked.

"Never mind. Make yourself beautiful."

Submissively, the Chinaman donned the girl's outfit, powdered his nose and completed the various details of his disguise. Joe made a dash down the stairs and returned with the report that Aunt Gertrude and the nurse were engaged in a lengthy argument as to whether certain tea leaves predicted a great catastrophe or a small legacy. The coast being clear, they went quietly downstairs and got out of the house without being seen.

"Where we go now?" repeated Tom Wat, who was getting suspicious.

"Come with us and see," said Frank.

He knew there would be violent objections on the part of their "girl friend" if Tom Wat knew that their destination was Louie Fong's laundry.

# CHAPTER XIX

## THE TRAP-DOOR

THEY were almost at the laundry before Tom
Wat realized their intention.

"No!" he exclaimed, holding back. "Me no
go in there. Velly bad place now."

Frank held the Chinaman firmly by the arm.

"You're a girl now, remember," he said.
"If you keep quiet they'll never suspect. Come
along."

Joe opened the door. Tom Wat was thrust
across the threshold before he could object
further. Once inside the door he realized that
it would be useless to resist, so he made himself as inconspicuous as possible in a corner.

There was no one behind the counter. The
laundry was dark for the window-blinds were
drawn, but from beyond the new partition the
boys saw the gleam of an electric light.

They heard voices from behind the half wall.
The boys, however, could not understand what
was being said for the unseen occupants of the
laundry were talking in Chinese.

One voice they recognized. It startled them.

It was the voice of Sam Lee—the gentle old Chinaman who had previously owned the shop.

Evidently the men in the back room were too engrossed in their conversation to hear the entry of the boys. No one came out to the counter.

Sam Lee was evidently excited. His voice was high and shrill. He talked volubly. Then another voice broke in. It was the voice of Louie Fong, smooth and sinister, deadly with menace. He said only a few words and then Sam Lee broke into excited speech again.

"What are they saying?" whispered Frank to Tom Wat.

"Sam Lee askee why Louie Fong make plenty changes in laundly," replied the Chinaman in a low voice.

Suddenly Frank nudged his brother.

"Look!" he exclaimed.

Into the gloomy area behind the counter emerged a gaunt, gray shadow. It was a dog, a huge Russian wolfhound. The boys recognized the animal at once.

It was the beast that had attacked them when they were hiding in the bushes near "Lantern Land." The animal paid them scant attention, however, merely nosing about the back of the laundry, then padding silently behind the partition once more.

The boys were startled by this discovery. It

was evident that the dog belonged to Louie
Fong. Its appearance here was almost con-
clusive proof that Louie Fong had indeed been
the man who had hurled the knife at Tom Wat.

The conversation back of the partition was
becoming more lively. Shrill voices were
raised in angry argument. Tom Wat was listening intently, a puzzled frown upon his face.

"Louie Fong say he fix Sam Lee," he whispered to Frank.

They heard Sam Lee's voice, angry and excited. Suddenly the voice ended in a choking
cry. There was a scuffle, then someone crashed
against the partition. They heard a snarl
from the huge dog. There were noises of a
struggle beyond the wall. Suddenly the gleam
of electric light from the back of the laundry
disappeared.

Tom Wat slipped swiftly toward the door.
He opened it and gestured urgently to the boys,
who followed him out into the street.

Tom Wat walked rapidly away. He was
shaking with fear. As for the Hardy boys,
they did not know what to think.

"What happened?" asked Frank, grabbing
the Chinaman by the arm. "What did Louie
Fong say?"

Tom Wat was almost too terrified for speech.
After a while, however, he blurted out:

"Mebbe Louie Fong killee Sam Lee."

"You think Louie has murdered him?" gasped Joe.

"Much talk. Sam Lee velly mad. Louie Fong tell him shut up. Mebbe Sam Lee dead now. Velly bad man, Louie Fong."

The boys were aghast. They did not know whether to go back to the laundry or to notify the police. Joe was in favor of the latter course.

"For all we know," he said, "Sam Lee may have been murdered. We ought to tell an officer right away."

Tom Wat objected to this vigorously. He did not want to be mixed up in the affair. If Sam Lee was murdered and the police arrested Louie Fong his own life would be in grave danger, he told them.

"After all," reflected Frank, "we aren't sure. If we bring the police into this and there is nothing wrong, it will spoil everything."

They turned and looked back toward the laundry.

"I wish we knew what happened back of that partition," muttered Joe.

At that moment the door of the shop opened, and a man stepped out. The boys stared in amazement. It was none other than Sam Lee. The old Chinaman came out onto the pavement, looked around, thrust his hands into his pockets and shuffled off down the street.

"Come on!" said Joe. "Let's go and ask him what happened."

But Frank had another plan.

"Louie Fong may be watching," he said. "If he sees us talking to Sam Lee he'll be suspicious. You trail him, Joe, and when you're out of sight of the laundry you can talk to him."

"And what are you going to do?"

"I want to find out what's going on in that place."

Joe was dubious.

"I think that laundry is a good place to leave alone," he said. "However, you're the doctor. I'm going after Sam Lee."

He strode away and hurried after the Chinaman.

"What you do now?" asked Tom Wat nervously.

"We're going back there."

Again Tom Wat objected. He was greatly shaken by the fright he had received and although the appearance of Sam Lee, safe and sound, had served to quiet his fears he did not view with delight the prospect of again entering the building. Frank, however, explained that they would merely go in and ask for the washing.

"I'll ask Louie Fong if he has seen Sam Lee lately. I wonder what he'll say."

Reluctantly, Tom Wat agreed to go with him.

He made no secret of the fact that the expedition was against his better judgment.

They approached the building once more and went inside. Again, however, the place seemed to be deserted. Louie Fong did not come to the counter. There was no sign of the huge dog. The place was in absolute silence.

A thought flashed into Frank's mind. Perhaps Louie Fong had been the victim of the quarrel following the argument between the two Chinamen. Perhaps he had been attacked by Sam Lee.

He rapped sharply on the counter. There was no answer.

"Louie!" he shouted.

Still no answer. He turned to Tom Wat.

"That's queer," said Frank.

Tom Wat's eyes were round with fear. He expressed the thought that had been in Frank's mind.

"Mebbe Louie Fong dead!" he gasped.

With that he turned, wrenched open the door and bolted out of the shop. He ran out into the street and headed for the Hardy house as if the terrible Louie Fong were at his heels.

Frank did not follow. Having gone this far he was not prepared to give up. He wanted to know what had happened behind the partition.

Frank knocked on the counter again.

"Louie Fong!" he shouted. "Are you there, Louie Fong?"

He heard only the echo of his own voice. Frank called again and when there was still no response he went toward the little door at the side of the counter, unfastened the catch and stepped inside.

Quietly, he made his way toward the partition. If anyone came in he could truthfully say that he had come for the laundry and that when no one appeared to serve him he had gone back to investigate.

Frank came around the partition into the little room at the back. But he did not find Louie Fong. He saw only a wooden table and two chairs. He spied a door, however, which evidently led into premises at the back of the establishment.

Frank hesitated a moment. Should he go on?

He tried the door. It was not locked, and swung silently open. He peeped into the room beyond. It, too, was deserted. The place was plainly furnished with a small stove, a table, a cot and a few chairs, and had evidently been Sam Lee's kitchen and living quarters.

Frank was puzzled. He could not believe that Louie Fong had gone away leaving the laundry unlocked and deserted.

"Louie Fong!" he called out again.

Still there was no answer.

He was tempted to go back, yet the mystery of the place intrigued him. He had a vague impression that he could hear voices in the distance. There was another door but he was sure it opened on the lane at the back of the laundry.

However, he decided to investigate it, so stepped toward the door.

Then suddenly he felt himself falling. The floor had opened beneath his feet. Frank uttered a loud cry. He strove wildly to retain his balance. But he had stepped directly upon a trap-door that fell open beneath his weight.

He plunged into the darkness beneath.

# CHAPTER XX

## SAM LEE'S STORY

As JOE HARDY hurried down the street in pursuit of Sam Lee he thought it would be an easy matter to overtake the old Chinaman. When he came to the end of the block, however, he looked vainly in all directions without catching sight of Sam Lee. The man had disappeared.

"He must be able to make himself invisible," said Joe in chagrin, for he knew Sam Lee had not had time in which to walk the length of the next block. Yet the old fellow had vanished as if the earth had swallowed him up. There was no one in sight but a small boy sitting on the curb.

"Did you see a Chinaman come this way?" Joe asked the youngster.

The boy looked up. He pointed to a nearby lane.

Joe dashed down the narrow thoroughfare. It struck him then that Sam Lee was afraid of being followed and was trying to shake off any possible pursuit.

161

He did not see his quarry in the lane but when he came out into the next street he caught a fleeting glimpse of the old Chinaman just disappearing around the corner. Sam Lee was headed toward the docks.

Joe quickened his pace, then broke into a run. At the corner he was in time to see Sam Lee near the waterfront. The old fellow had evidently concluded that he had eluded any possible pursuit by now, for he was shuffling along at an ordinary gait. Joe hurried up behind him.

"Sam Lee!" he said softly.

The old man turned quickly. There was a frightened light in his eyes, but when he recognized Joe Hardy he looked relieved.

"Hello!" he said. "How are you, boy?"

Sam Lee had been in the laundry business in Bayport for years. He spoke good English with only a trace of an accent.

"What's the matter, Sam? Have you sold your shop? We miss you."

"Yes," he said. "I do not run the laundry any more. I have rented it."

"To Louie Fong?"

"Yes. To Louie Fong."

"He's a queer customer, that fellow," said Joe. "I don't think he's a laundryman any more than I am. What's behind this business, Sam Lee?"

"You ask questions," said Sam Lee thoughtfully. "Why?"

"Look here, Sam," replied Joe. "You've known me for a long time. You know you can trust me. I've been acquainted with you for a good many years, too. What made you quit the laundry business so suddenly without saying a word to anyone?"

Sam Lee was silent for a moment.

"Louie Fong wanted to rent my place. He offered me a good price. I took it. That is all."

"There's more to it than that, Sam. You can't fool me. Frank and I have been trying to get some information about this Louie Fong. He's mixed up in some queer business. What do you know about it?"

Sam Lee looked cautiously about.

"It is dangerous for me to talk about Louie Fong," he answered.

"What connection," asked Joe abruptly, "has Louie Fong with Orrin North?"

Sam Lee's eyelids flickered. He could not conceal his surprise at this question.

"How do you know," he asked, "that Louie Fong and Mr. North are working together?"

"I'm sure that something queer is going on but I don't know what it is."

"It is not my affair," returned Sam Lee. "I am an honest man."

"Then it's a dishonest business that they're in?" said Joe quickly.

Sam Lee saw that he had given himself away. But he was discreet.

"It is not my affair," he repeated.

"And yet you rent your laundry to Louie Fong?" insisted Joe.

"I could not help that. Louie Fong is a cruel man, a hard master. If I do not do as he says —it would mean trouble," and the gentle old Chinaman shrugged his shoulders eloquently.

Joe remembered what Orrin North had said about the accusations levelled against him. He hazarded a question.

"Are Louie Fong and Orrin North smuggling Chinamen into the country?"

Sam Lee started. He looked hastily around, as if fearful that someone might have overheard Joe's remark.

"Who told you that?" he demanded quietly.

"Never mind. But I want to know more about it. Is that the game they're in?"

"I may speak safely? You will tell no one that you talked to me?"

"Of course," Joe assured him. "Everything is in confidence."

"Louie Fong is indeed in league with Orrin North," he admitted. "They are smuggling Chinamen into the country. Louie Fong pays North to bring them here in his ships. These men think they will make their fortunes once they are in America. But when they reach here they find that they are the slaves of Louie Fong."

"How is that?"

"It is very simple," continued Sam Lee. "These Chinamen know they have not entered the country according to law. They know that they will be deported if they are found out. They are afraid of that. When they are taken off the ships they are sent at once to Louie Fong. He finds work for them. But always he demands part of their wages."

"Until they have paid what they owe him for bringing them into the country?"

Sam Lee smiled bitterly.

"They would save money if they paid the head tax in the first place. They always keep handing part of their wages to Louie Fong. Year after year."

"But that's sheer blackmail!" exclaimed Joe in amazement at this story of cold-blooded extortion.

"If they object, if they do not pay—then the authorities receive word to investigate them. Then they are deported. But they do not refuse to pay."

Joe realized that he had stumbled upon a secret of tremendous importance. Orrin North and the rascally Chinaman were leagued in a great scheme of smuggling and blackmail in which they mercilessly exploited the poor coolies who fell into their clutches. Orrin North, then, was really guilty of the very crime of which he claimed he had been unjustly accused.

With a shock Joe realized why his own father had been employed by Orrin North to investigate the rumors of smuggling. Fenton Hardy was merely being used as a foil in case the authorities should investigate. Joe saw that his father had been skillfully trapped into becoming an unwitting assistant of criminals. With Fenton Hardy ostensibly working to run down the smugglers on behalf of Orrin North the authorities would take North's innocence for granted. Fenton Hardy's reputation for honesty would take care of that.

But if the truth came out—what then? His father's reputation would be ruined. It would be held that he had been a mere tool of the smuggling gang. The more he considered it the more Joe saw that the situation was serious. With all his heart he wished he could get in touch with his father before anything further developed.

Sam Lee touched him gently on the arm.

"You will tell no one you were talking to me?" said the Chinaman.

"My brother. But no one else."

"I am in hiding. No one must know I have been in Bayport."

"Where are you hiding, Sam? Where can I find you if I want to get in touch with you?"

"Up the river." Sam Lee then described to Joe the location of the refuge he had chosen. "Should you need me," he said, "you can find me there. I will help you if I can."

"You don't like Louie Fong, then?"

Sam Lee's face hardened.

"I should like to see him thrown in jail," he returned. "He is a cruel man. But I dare not fight against him myself. He would kill me."

"And Orrin North?"

"He would not kill. But he is a bad man. He should be in jail, too."

"And that's where he'll land if Frank and I have anything to say about it," declared Joe, as he thought of the dangerous position into which his father had evidently been maneuvered.

Then he remembered Tom Wat. The plight of the little Chinaman was a constant source of worry as long as he remained in the Hardy home. Joe knew that as soon as Aunt Gertrude was able to be up and about again it would be only a matter of time before the presence of the secret guest would be discovered.

"Do you know Tom Wat?" he asked.

"Yes," said Sam Lee, "I know him well. Like me, he does not like Louie Fong."

"Louie Fong has tried to kill him. Twice. He is hidden at our house."

"Ah?" said Sam Lee in surprise.

"We won't be able to keep him there much longer. You say you have a good hiding place up the river. Now, how about taking Tom Wat up there with you? He'll be safe enough then."

Sam Lee considered the matter.

"Tom Wat is a good boy," he said. "If you can send him to me I will see that he shares my hiding place."

"That's fine!" exclaimed Joe, greatly relieved. "Frank and I will see that he is taken to your secret house as soon as possible. It's mighty good of you, Sam."

"Friend must help friend," murmured Sam Lee, as he turned to go. "We shall meet again, boy. I have told you where I may be found. I have told you what I know about Louie Fong. I trust you."

"You won't regret it, Sam Lee," Joe assured him warmly.

# CHAPTER XXI

## PERIL UNDERGROUND

WHEN he crashed through the hidden trap-door Frank Hardy plunged into the basement beneath. He was stunned by the impact of his fall but he was not knocked unconscious. For a while he lay sprawled on the floor, trying to recover his breath.

Then he sat up, felt his bruises and satisfied himself that no bones were broken. He was badly shaken. It was a miracle, he told himself, that he had not broken his neck.

But Frank was not yet out of the woods. He could see the opening in the floor above but it was beyond his reach. When he looked around the gloomy little cellar into which he had tumbled he saw nothing that would help him reach the trap-door.

He picked himself up and began to explore the underground room. He had gone hardly three steps before he stumbled against an object on the floor.

Frank started back in astonishment. A human figure lay among the rubbish at his feet,

Frank knelt down. In the dim light he could just distinguish the man's face. It was that of Louie Fong!

His first thought was that the evil man was dead. The prone figure did not stir. With a shock he remembered the sounds of struggle behind the partition. Had Sam Lee murdered Louie Fong?

Then he heard a deep groan. Louie Fong's lips twitched. He stirred slightly.

Frank withdrew into the dark shadows of the cellar.

Louie Fong groaned again. His eyes opened. He lay there for a while, then sat up painfully and rubbed his head. He had either been dealt a severe blow on the head or else he had been knocked senseless by his fall through the trap-door. He was groggy.

At last the Chinaman struggled to his feet. He muttered to himself, still rubbing his head. Unsteadily, he lurched across the cellar. Then he tugged at an iron ring set into the wall.

Frank had noticed this ring but had paid scant attention to it. It had not struck him that it might indicate an exit.

Louie Fong drew the ring toward him, and silently part of the wall gave way. A door swung slowly open and revealed a dim passage beyond.

The Chinaman stumbled down the passage.

He was so groggy, however, that he did not shut the door behind him. Swiftly Frank followed.

The passage was so dark that the boy had little fear of being seen, but he kept at a respectful distance behind. The Chinaman reached a flight of stairs and ascended.

Frank was puzzled. He knew that the laundry was only a small building. This passage doubtless led beneath the adjacent lot. Then he remembered that there was an empty store beside the laundry. This, doubtless, was the place to which the alley would open.

Louie Fong went up the stairs, opened another door and went on. Frank followed in the semi-darkness, and reached the doorway in time to see the Chinaman enter a room, which was furnished in Oriental style. There were a few screens, a hanging lantern, a mirror upon the wall. Beyond the room was a half-open door, through which Frank could hear a confused murmur of voices.

Louie Fong stood at the door for a moment, peering into the room beyond. Then he turned and looked at himself in the mirror. Frank saw that he was badly battered. The Chinaman had a black eye and there was a big bruise on his forehead.

The Chinaman studied his reflection in the glass. Then, instead of going into the other room he stepped toward a side door, opened it and disappeared.

Frank hesitated. Should he follow Louie Fong, or should he make an investigation of that other room?

It occurred to him that the Chinaman did not want to face the others because of his battered appearance. Frank stepped in quietly. Then he heard a familiar voice.

"Come on, now! Kick in with that money, every man of you. Ten dollars each."

The voice was that of Orrin North!

"Ten dollars each and I want it right away," North's voice continued. "If I don't get it you'll find yourselves in jail. And then you'll be packed back to China in a hurry."

A whimpering voice replied:

"Ten dolla' all I got."

"What's that to me?"

There was a gabbled mutter of protest in Chinese. Another voice said:

"Why don't you leave them alone, North? They've already paid you. Why make them cough up more?"

"You mind your own business," snarled North. "I'm running this show."

Frank crept forward, and peered into the next room.

There were a dozen men in the place. Three Chinamen sat at a table with two sailors. Over in a corner crouched a group of frightened coolies, wretchedly clad. It was evident that they had just disembarked. Orrin North towered over them, his red face brutal, his hand extended.

"Hurry up!" he rasped. "Ten dollars from each of you. If you don't want to go back to China you'd better hand it over."

Meekly, one of the coolies took a few worn bills from his pocket and gave them to the ship owner. The others, muttering their objections, followed suit.

"That's better," growled North, stuffing the money into his pocket. "You'll work harder if you haven't any money to start with."

He laughed callously and strode over to the table, where he sat down. The coolies eyed him, frightened.

"Well," declared Orrin North, rubbing his hands briskly, "that's a good day's work."

"You shouldn't have taken all their money," grunted one of the sailors.

"Why not?" barked North. "I was lucky to get in here before Louie Fong got at them. He'd have taken it if he'd got to them first, you can depend on it."

He chuckled.

"Mighty good joke on Louie," he said complacently.

"I wonder where Louie is, anyway," asked

the sailor. "It ain't like him to stay away so long."

"It cost him fifty bucks and serves him right," laughed North.

"You're smart, Mr. North," said the other sailor admiringly.

"Of course I'm smart," agreed North. "I'm a rich man and you don't get rich unless you're smart, let me tell you. And you don't stay long in this smuggling game unless you're mighty smart. But I've got that all fixed up. There's only one man could trip me up and I have him out of the way."

"Who's that?"

"Fenton Hardy."

"The detective!"

"Some detective," laughed North. "Why, say—as a detective, this fellow Hardy is a joke. I've got him helping me and he doesn't know it. And besides, he's out of town. Things can move nicely now. I think I'm clever to get a famous fellow like that out from under my nose."

He laughed, slapping the table. The sailors, who were evidently in his employ and fearful of offending their master, laughed also. The Chinamen said nothing.

"Yes, sir," declared North, "it takes a clever man to outwit Fenton Hardy and the government all at the same time."

Suddenly Frank became aware that he was not the only watcher. Partly hidden by some paper flowers on the opposite wall he noticed a narrow slit in the woodwork.

Beyond this slit he saw a pair of eyes! The eyes were fixed intently on Orrin North.

"Yep!" gloated the ship owner. "It takes a smart man to beat me at this game. How long would Louie Fong last without me? Why, he wouldn't last a minute. Who thought of freezing Sam Lee out of the laundry and putting Louie in there? Why, it was me."

"That was a good stunt, all right."

"And who thought of buying this empty store and fixing up a passage to the laundry? Me, again. The police wouldn't get wise to this place in a hundred years."

Suddenly one of the Chinamen leaned across the table, and spoke sharply to Orrin North. With a mutter of alarm the man swung around in his chair. He looked directly toward the slit in the wall. He saw the eyes!

North's hand flew to his pocket. He wrenched out a revolver, raised it and fired. Instantly the room was in an uproar. The two sailors sprang up from their chairs. The coolies gabbled in terror. The other China-men rushed for the door.

"A spy!" roared North. He fired again. But the mysterious eyes had vanished.

"Come on!" shouted one of the sailors. "We'll catch him outside."

"No!" yelled North. "We can't have everybody running out of here. The police would get wise. I'll go myself."

He strode across the room, wrenched open a door and disappeared. Frank was afraid the search might result in his own discovery, so he leaped quickly toward the door through which Louie Fong had vanished. Fortunately it was not locked. He opened it and ran out.

It opened on a short, dark hall. Frank sped through the gloom, raced to the door at the end of the hall, flung it open. He found himself outside.

There, huddled in a heap at the bottom of the step he found Louie Fong. The Chinaman lay unconscious.

Frank knelt down and shook the prostrate figure. The man opened his eyes and muttered something in a dull voice.

Was Louie Fong the man who had been spying through the slit in the wall? And had Orrin North shot him?

Frank dragged the Chinaman to his feet. Louie Fong was scarcely able to stand.

At that moment Joe dashed around the corner of the building.

"What's the matter?" he gasped. "I went back to the laundry and you weren't there. I heard shots." Then he saw the Chinaman.

"Louie Fong," said Frank swiftly. "Quick! Help me get him out of here. He's been shot or slugged. Hurry."

Without another word Joe grabbed the Oriental by the arm. They hustled him around the side of the store and out into the alley at the back. Frank was in momentary fear lest they run into Orrin North, but the ship owner's search had evidently taken him to the other side of the building.

"Where shall we take him?" asked Joe.

"Down to the garage. Let's put him in our car," snapped Frank. "He's so groggy he doesn't know what he's doing."

By making Louie Fong a captive, reflected Frank, they would gain great headway in their campaign against the smuggling ring. And, whatever had happened to him, the Chinaman scarcely seemed to be in his right senses. He staggered and would have fallen if they had not been holding him by the arms.

Fortunately they met no one in the alley. It ran parallel to High Street and brought them to the rear of their own garage. They hustled Louie Fong into the building.

"Let's look him over and see if he's wounded," Frank suggested. "Orrin North shot at a man who was watching through the wall——"

"Orrin North!" exclaimed Joe in astonishment. "Where did all this happen?"

"I'll tell you later. I've had some adventures since you left me."

"And I've picked up some information."

Louie Fong sagged suddenly. He had lapsed into unconsciousness again. Though he was not wounded, they found a huge bump on his head, and Frank judged that this was the cause of his condition.

"Sam Lee must have walloped him on the head and shoved him into the cellar. He came to, all right, but he went under again," said Frank. "Here, we'll put him in the car."

They hoisted the limp figure into the roadster.

"But who was the peeping stranger?" exclaimed Frank in bewilderment.

# CHAPTER XXII

## SAM LEE'S HIDING PLACE

"What are we to do with this prize package?" asked Joe, motioning toward the unconscious Louie Fong.

"That's another problem. When I saw him on the doorstep I just grabbed him. If we can only manage to keep him prisoner somewhere and force him to tell us something about his dealings with Orrin North we'll be making progress."

"I know something about his dealings with North," said Joe. "I talked to Sam Lee."

"What did he say?" asked Frank eagerly.

Joe then told him of his interview with the old Chinaman and of Sam Lee's story that Orrin North and Louie Fong were leagued in a smuggling enterprise.

"That checks exactly with what I learned!" Frank exclaimed, and he told Joe of his adventures in the laundry, of his fall through the trap-door and his discovery of the passage leading into the adjacent building.

"We've stumbled on an important secret, no

179

doubt of that," declared Joe. "We can't let Louie Fong out of our hands. But where are we to keep him?"

"You said Sam Lee has a hideout up the river," exclaimed Frank in excitement. "There's the very place. We can take him there, tie him up and leave Sam Lee to watch him for us."

"Good idea! I never thought of that. His friends won't find him there in a hurry, I'll be bound."

"But first of all there's something I want to do."

"What is it?"

"I'd like to know more about the stranger who was spying on Orrin North in the secret room," said Frank.

"Why, he'll be miles away by now."

"He may be. But not his footprints."

"I see what you mean. You want to check up on any tracks he may have left around the door."

In case Louie Fong should recover consciousness the boys resurrected an old pair of handcuffs—souvenirs of one of their previous cases—and clapped them on the wrists of the unconscious prisoner.

Frank took tape and paper with him, slipped out of the garage and retraced his steps down the alley. He passed the laundry. There was no sign of life. He went on to the apparently deserted store beyond. No one was in sight. The windows were boarded up, and to all appearances no human being had entered the building in months. Of course Frank knew otherwise.

He went around to the side of the store, examined the earth beneath the windows, and at last he found what he sought. Two footprints, clear and distinct in the sand.

Frank knelt down and quickly took measurements of the telltale marks. He jotted them down and hurriedly left the scene. Not five minutes had elapsed before he returned to the garage.

"Where are those other figures, Joe?" he asked.

"The measurements of the other footprints? Why, they're up in our room. But we don't need them. I can remember them. You don't mean to say you think they're the same?"

"I'm sure of it," and Frank recited the measurements he had just taken.

"Why, they're exactly the same!"

The boys stared at each other in profound amazement.

"Then," said Frank, "that man who left the footprints under the window——"

"Was the same man who spied on Orrin North today."

"And the same man who spied on Louie Fong and Orrin North at the garage."

"I wonder," observed Joe, "if the first Sidney Pebbles is still mixed up in this affair."

"Well, we won't get anywhere by wondering about it," declared his brother. "Our problem right now is to get Louie Fong up to Sam Lee's hideout and see that he's put under guard."

He jumped into the driver's seat, while Joe clambered in at the other side. Louie Fong, still unconscious and handcuffed, was wedged between them. Frank ran the car out of the garage.

"Where now?"

"The boathouse."

Sam Lee's hiding place was on the Willow River. According to Joe's description of the place Frank knew that it would be possible to motor within a few miles of the place, but that meant a long walk with their prisoner. He did not relish the prospect of dragging Louie Fong through several miles of bush country when the place could be reached directly by water.

The Hardy boys owned a motorboat which they called *The Sleuth*. It had been purchased out of prize money they had earned for solving one of the mysteries they had tackled. The craft would be useful at this time.

When they reached the boathouse they saw a familiar figure tinkering at the engine of a motorboat near the dock. It was the *Napoli*, owned by Tony Prito, an Italian-American lad who was one of their chums. As their car came to a stop Tony looked up and saw them.

"Hi!" he shouted and stepped out of his craft. "Where have you two been all week?"

He came toward them. As he passed one of the boathouses he looked inside and called out:

"Here they are, Chet. Come along."

Chet Morton emerged at a bound.

"Well! Well!" he said, grinning. "If it isn't our old pals, the Hardy boys. Where've you been all summer? Spending your holidays in Europe or somewhere?"

Tony Prito laughed.

"Chet was just saying that you fellows have been up to something."

"I'll say they have," grumbled Chet. "Got me started on a swell mystery and just when I was giving them some real help they left me out in the cold. Then they started going around with a swell looking girl and began giving all their old friends the air."

Suddenly he spied Louie Fong in the car.

"Great suffering hoptoads!" he yelped. "What have you got there? A mummy?"

Tony Prito's eyes bulged.

"Is it real?" he squeaked.

"Of course it's real," said Frank, getting out of the car. "Come on, Chet. You've been complaining that we've been freezing you out of this mystery. You're in it now. You too, Tony.''

''Good!'' exclaimed Tony, beaming with pleasure. ''I like mysteries.''

''Say!'' muttered Chet, staring at the unconscious Chinaman. ''That looks mighty like Louie Fong.''

''It *is* Louie Fong,'' said Joe.

Chet gulped.

''I don't know as I care for this mystery as much as I thought I would,'' he said. ''That man is a bad actor, by all accounts. What have you done to him? Is he dead or chloroformed?''

''Neither,'' returned Frank. ''He's knocked out, that's all, and he's likely to come to at any minute.''

''In that case,'' said Chet, ''I'll be seeing you at Sunday School the day after tomorrow.''

He began to walk away, but Frank collared his chum.

''You want to be involved in mysteries,'' he reminded Chet firmly. ''You're in one now. Help us get Louie into our boat.''

''My boat's all ready,'' said Tony Prito. ''Use mine. Where are you going?''

''Up the Willow River.''

''Load him in, then, and come along.''

Tony went on ahead and scrambled into the *Napoli* while the boys followed, carrying Louie

Fong. They dumped him into the boat. Tony took the wheel and Chet cast off. The engine throbbed and in a few moments the swift craft was speeding out into Barmet Bay.

Their journey across the bay and up the Willow River was uneventful. Louie Fong still remained unconscious. Chet and Tony were wildly curious as to how the Chinaman had fallen into the hands of the Hardy boys and as to the reasons for his abduction. When Frank and Joe told them some of their adventures they were more than astonished at the maze of intrigue and crime in which Orrin North and Louie Fong were involved.

"This is big stuff!" exclaimed Chet seriously. "Boy, I'm glad that rascal is unconscious. And handcuffed, too. If he woke up he'd start raising ructions."

"He's pretty harmless right now," said Frank. "And once we get to Sam Lee's place I think he'll be in safe keeping until we have time to attend to Orrin North."

They found Sam Lee's hiding place without difficulty, following the directions the old Chinaman had given Joe. The place was on a branch of the river and so cleverly concealed that they would never have suspected its presence if they had not known where to look.

They found Sam Lee sitting in the doorway of an old shack in the bush beside the creek.

"Ah!" he said when he saw Joe. "You come soon."

Then, when he spied the limp figure of Louie Fong, he drew back with an exclamation of alarm.

"What has happened?" he asked tensely. "Did I kill him?"

"I thought so," laughed Frank. "It was *you* who knocked him on the head in the laundry."

Sam Lee nodded.

"He insulted me. I struck him when he tried to choke me. He fell down. I took him over to the trap-door and dropped him into the cellar."

"He isn't dead," Joe assured him. "But we thought he might as well be kept under guard. That's why we brought him here."

Sam Lee shook his head doubtfully.

"You are brave boys," he said, "to kidnap so big a criminal as Louie Fong."

"It didn't take much bravery," said Frank. "He hasn't recovered from that wallop yet. He woke up a couple of times but caved in again. We put handcuffs on him, so he's harmless even if he does wake up."

"Louie Fong is never harmless," said Sam Lee. "He is always dangerous. Like a rattlesnake."

It was easily seen, however, that the old Chinaman was pleased at Louie Fong's capture.

They brought the prisoner into the shack. He muttered uneasily as they carried him, and Chet jumped nervously to one side.

"Look out!" he exclaimed. "He's waking up now."

Louie Fong's eyes opened. He stared about him, then narrowed his eyes suddenly as he realized that he was in an unfamiliar place and in strange hands. For the moment, however, he said nothing.

The boys put him on Sam Lee's cot, where he sat for a moment, shaking his head. Then he moved his arms and discovered that his wrists were handcuffed. With a wild yell he sprang to his feet, his evil face distorted with fury.

"Let me go!" he screeched. "What place you bling me? Let me go!"

He broke into a wild tirade of threats. He would kill them, he said, unless they set him free. He flung himself about the tiny cabin, kicking at the walls, trying to get at his captors. Frank and Tony Prito seized him and shoved him back onto the cot.

"Close that door, Chet!" snapped Frank.

"I was just going to," gasped Chet.

As a matter of fact, he was halfway through the doorway at the time. Chet had intended making a quiet departure, but he meekly closed the door and returned.

Louie Fong raved. He was furious with anger. His inky eyes were fixed on Sam Lee and he rasped out a torrent of threats in Chinese. Sam Lee turned pale.

"Don't worry," said Frank. "He'll quiet down when he sees it's of no use."

He spoke to Louie Fong.

"Look here!" he said. "We've learned a few things about you and North. We're going to break up this smuggling racket of yours. In the meantime, you're going to stay here. By the time we're ready to let you go back to Bayport you'll find that the game is up."

But, as Sam Lee had said, Louie Fong was always dangerous. The Chinaman's eyes glinted. He crouched on the cot, his hands behind his back. He appeared to be listening intently.

"You and Orrin North tricked my father," Frank continued. "We're going to get word to him and see that he learns the facts of the case."

"What's that?" asked Tony Prito suddenly.

Chet Morton jumped convulsively. Sam Lee turned and gazed at the door.

Tap . . . tap . . . tap.

There was a strange rapping going on. Louie Fong's face was transformed by a malicious grin.

"Someone at the door," whispered Joe.

## CHAPTER XXIII

### CHAN

THE strange tapping continued.

"Open it a bit and see who is there, Chet," said Frank.

"Maybe if we stay quiet he'll go away," Chet whispered.

Frank shook his head. In fear and trembling, then, Chet approached the door, and opened it a mere trifle. Suddenly Louie Fong spoke.

"Chan!" he said softly.

No sooner had he uttered the word than there was a frenzied snarl. A heavy body launched itself at the door. Chet was hurled on his back by the impact, and a gaunt gray form leaped over him.

It was Chan, the ferocious wolfhound of Louie Fong!

Instantly the shack was in confusion. The beast sprang straight at Frank. At the same moment Louie Fong rose from the cot with a wild yell. A quick wrench and the handcuffs clattered to the floor. All the time he had been sitting on the cot the wily Oriental had been working his wrists free of the rusty shackles.

Frank dodged as the dog leaped at him and the brute crashed against the wall. Sam Lee uttered a cry of despair. Tony Prito snatched up a stick and hurled it at Chan. Joe plunged at Louie Fong.

But Chan guarded his master. The huge dog whirled about and faced the group, fangs bared, eyes glaring. It snapped and snarled, threatening all within reach. Louie Fong deftly evaded Joe's rush and leaped toward the open door. One spring, and he vanished.

"After him!" yelled Frank, bounding outside.

He was brought up short as Chan, with a snarl of fury, raced ahead of him, wheeled and forced him back into the cabin. The animal growled menacingly, as he covered his master's retreat.

The boys were in a panic. Louie Fong had escaped and they were powerless to give pursuit. Moreover, they knew well the gravity of their danger once the Chinaman was at large again.

Tony Prito grabbed up the stick again. He flung it at the dog. The weapon missed its mark and flew over the animal's head but Chan yelped and backed away. A moment later, with a final howl, he fled into the bushes.

Sam Lee was gibbering with fear and excitement. The escape of his old enemy had left him in a pitiable state. Chet was beyond speech.

Frank and Joe rushed out of the shack. They heard a crashing in the bushes.

"After him!" shouted Frank. "He went this way."

They plunged into the undergrowth, Tony Prito close on their heels. They followed the direction of the sounds and a moment later came within sight of the dog. The great gray shape flashed in the bushes, then vanished again. Somewhere ahead was Louie Fong.

Joe circled around toward the creek, suspecting that Louie Fong might make his way to the boat. Tony Prito made a wide detour in the opposite direction. Chet, his first qualms having passed, hustled out of the shack and made himself very busy by tripping over bushes, plunging aimlessly here and there, shouting wildly, and carefully covering all the ground that the others had already searched.

They did not recapture Louie Fong. The bush was too dense and the Chinaman was too shrewd. After half an hour of vain search the boys were forced to admit defeat. Louie Fong and the wolfhound had escaped.

They returned to the shack, where Sam Lee was waiting for them anxiously.

"He was too quick for us, Sam. He made a clean getaway. He's probably heading back to Bayport by now."

The old man looked frightened.

"I am lost," he said simply. "Louie Fong will surely kill me now."

"You're in no danger," they assured him. "We'll look after you."

Sam Lee did not share their confidence, for he could not forget the terrible threats Louie Fong had hurled at him in the cabin.

"I can stay here no longer. He knows my hiding place."

"Yes, I guess you'll have to move away from here," Joe agreed. "I'm sorry, Sam Lee. It was our fault. We shouldn't have brought Louie Fong here."

"You are not to blame," said the old man gently. "If all had gone well it was the best thing to do. Who could have foreseen that the dog would trail him here?"

"And who could have known that the villain was getting rid of those handcuffs all the time you were talking to him?" spoke up Chet.

"We didn't put them on tightly enough. He managed to squeeze his hands through them all right."

"Now we're *all* in a fix," muttered Chet. "I wonder if my aunt up in Vermont would let me go and visit her on her farm for a few weeks.

I could catch the night train. Louie Fong would never chase me all the way to Vermont, would he?"

The others laughed. Chet was obviously frightened within an inch of his life.

"You might as well stay in Bayport," said Joe. "You wouldn't be any safer from Louie Fong if you went to the North Pole."

"I hope I have a nice funeral," groaned Chet comically. "To think of a promising lad like me being cut off in his prime. I wonder which of us will go first."

"I don't think he even saw you," scoffed Tony Prito. "He doesn't know you exist. You certainly weren't much in evidence during that rumpus in the shack."

"I thought I'd be more valuable if I sat down quietly and figured out a plan," replied Chet weakly, "but everything moved so fast I didn't have time."

"Well, you'd better think up a plan right now," said Frank. "What are we going to do with Sam Lee? We'll have to hide him in some safe place, that's certain."

"You've come to the right shop for an idea," answered Chet. "I know the very place. Safe as a church."

"Where?" they asked.

"Your boathouse."

"That's a real idea," applauded Joe. "I

wonder why we didn't think of hiding Tom Wat there.''

"Tom Wat!" exclaimed Chet. "What has Tom Wat got to do with this? Is he mixed up in it, too?"

Frank had almost given the secret of Tom Wat away. The boys had not told their chums the real identity of the pretty girl who had aroused Chet's curiosity.

"Never mind," he said hastily. "That's a good suggestion about the boathouse. It's close to our home so we can look in often and see that Sam Lee is comfortable. How about it, Sam Lee?"

"You may hide me wherever you wish," returned the old Chinaman mournfully. "It will be of no use. I am doomed. Louie Fong will find me out."

"I think we'll fix Louie Fong before he has a chance to do anything," said Joe cheerfully. "Let's get going. If we stick around here too long he may round up some of his friends and come back."

"I never thought of that," muttered Chet, and made a running hop-step-and-jump toward the motorboat.

They abandoned the shack at once and went down to the *Napoli*. Within a short time the speedy craft was racing down the river and heading toward the open bay.

It was dark when they crossed Barmet Bay and reached the boathouse, so they were able to smuggle Sam Lee into the building without being seen by anyone. The old Chinaman was grateful but he seemed to feel that the precautions were useless. Louie Fong, he said, would surely find his hiding place.

They made the old man as comfortable as they could. Tony Prito ran to his house nearby and came back with a supply of food from the kitchen. There were a few blankets that the boys had used on a camping trip and with these they improvised a bed.

"We'll drop in and see you before long," said Frank.

"And in case anything happens," said Chet, as he removed an object from the boat and put it on the floor beside Sam Lee, "just sound the alarm."

The object was the boat's klaxon.

Sam Lee smiled.

"You are very thoughtful," he said. "I am not afraid. What must come will come."

The boys left him. Near the Hardy home, Chet Morton and Tony Prito left the others, after Frank and Joe had promised to get in touch with them if they should happen to need their help.

"And don't forget that, either," instructed Chet. "I've been in this mystery at the start and in the middle and I don't want to miss the finish, if there is going to be any finish.''

"The finish would come quickly enough if we could only get in touch with Dad,'' said Frank. "I can't understand why he should stay away so long.''

"I have a hunch,'' remarked Joe, "that some of Orrin North's crowd are doing their best to keep him out of town.''

"Whatever the reason is, he isn't here so we must carry on alone,'' decided Frank.

They said goodbye to their chums and went into the house. The moment they entered the door they were aware that something had gone wrong. Upstairs they could hear the voice of Aunt Gertrude. She was highly excited—raving, in fact.

"Call the police! Call the police, Nurse!''

The boys rushed up the stairs. On the landing they encountered Nurse Cody, whose face was as white as the proverbial sheet.

"Get him out of here!'' Aunt Gertrude was clamoring. "We'll all be murdered in our beds. Get that man out of this house. Lock him up! Call the police before he gets away.''

"What's wrong, Mrs. Cody?''

Their first thought was that Louie Fong had invaded the house in search of them.

The nurse could scarcely speak. She gulped with terror.

"A—a man!" she gasped at last.

"A man? Where?" demanded Frank.

"I—I locked him up!" stammered the frightened woman.

"Get him out of the house this instant," wailed Aunt Gertrude.

The boys heard a violent pounding from the vicinity of a closet at the end of the hall.

"In there!" gasped Nurse Cody, as she pointed to the place where bedding was stored. In her hand she clutched a key.

Frank took the key and strode toward the door.

"Don't let him out!" shrieked the nurse. "He'll murder us all."

"It's a Chinaman!" screamed Aunt Gertrude from her room.

"A Chinaman!" exclaimed Joe.

As the boys advanced toward the closet door, the pounding became more violent than ever. There was certainly someone locked in there. Was the prisoner Louie Fong?

# CHAPTER XXIV

FRANK fitted the key into the lock.

"Don't open that door!" screamed Aunt Gertrude. "Get the police!"

The nurse fled to Aunt Gertrude's room and peeped out through the half-open door, ready to slam it shut at an instant's notice.

The pounding continued. Frank seized the knob, turned the key and stepped back.

Out tumbled Tom Wat, with the girl's hat down over one eye and the skirt dragging about his heels. The young man was nearly dead from excitement.

"Me aflaid of lady!" he babbled. "Muchee aflaid of lady. Lockee me up." He grabbed Frank by the sleeve.

The first shock of surprise having passed, the Hardy boys roared with laughter. Joe sat down on the floor, weak with mirth at the spectacle of the bedraggled and frightened Chinaman.

"Don't let him get away!" clamored Aunt Gertrude. "Sit on his head."

198

"Me muchee aflaid of lady!"

"And the lady is muchee aflaid of you, too," snorted Joe. "How on earth did they catch you, Tom?"

"Me get hungly. Me come down stailway. Lady catchee me. Lady shout, 'Whoops!' and glab me," related Tom Wat, shuddering at the recollection. "Me hide in closet. Lockee me up then."

Explanations, of course, were in order. Frank and Joe brought their trembling guest into Aunt Gertrude's room, vastly to the alarm of that lady and Nurse Cody. Then they explained how they had smuggled Tom Wat into the house to protect him from the insidious Louie Fong.

Aunt Gertrude, her fears allayed, scolded the boys for giving her such a fright. The scare, however, had done her good. She seemed more active than she had been since she entered the house. In fact, she seemed to forget that she was supposed to be ill.

"I never heard of such a thing!" she exclaimed. "A Chinaman in the room overhead all the time. If I'd known it I'd have died! I'd have simply up and died of sheer fright."

"Such goings-on!" sniffed Nurse Cody. "Scarin' two defenceless women out of their wits."

"Look what you did to Tom Wat, though,"

pointed out Frank. "He's a nervous wreck. He'll never be the same again."

When the excitement had died down the boys took the Chinaman to their room. There they told him of the happenings in the laundry, of the capture and escape of Louie Fong.

Tom Wat's face became grave.

"Velly bad!" he said. "Louie Fong makee much tlouble for you."

"We must make trouble for Louie Fong before he can get started. That's the only answer," said Frank.

"How?" asked Joe.

"I have an idea. If we go back to Fong's place we may be able to learn something. If he has returned we'll get the police to round up the whole crowd. We have evidence against Louie Fong and North, as it is."

Joe shook his head.

"If Louie Fong should see us, we're certainly done for."

"We'll go in disguise."

"Tom Wat is disguised. How about us?"

"I'll go with Tom Wat—as a Chinaman."

Frank proceeded to put his idea into execution. From a drawer he removed a box of grease paints that Fenton Hardy had discarded from his collection. Joe slipped downstairs to the little room off their father's office, where Fenton Hardy kept his collection of disguises.

He returned in a few minutes with a coat, trousers, slippers and queer, flat hat.

"The very thing!" said Joe proudly. "Dad used this outfit when he was investigating the tong wars in Chinatown, back in New York."

Frank sat down in front of the mirror. Swiftly he applied the grease paint. With the aid of Tom Wat he soon transformed himself into a very realistic Oriental.

"Where do I come in?" asked Joe.

"You trail Wat and me," returned his brother. "If we get into difficulties you can get help for us."

Tom Wat's attire was soon straightened out, and although he had many misgivings about returning to the neighborhood of Louie Fong's place he was persuaded to join the expedition.

"All set?" said Frank. "Let's go."

They slipped out of the house and made their way toward the alley. Here, in the darkness, they discussed their plans for a moment. Then Frank and Tom Wat set out together, Joe remaining in the shadows. Presently he followed them at a respectful distance.

Louie Fong's laundry was in darkness, so they went on toward the apparently deserted store. Suddenly Frank stopped.

"Someone there already," he whispered to Tom Wat, who peered into the gloom.

Against the side of the building they saw a

dark shadow. A man was prowling about beneath the windows. He advanced a pace, crouched down, appeared to be listening. Then he moved forward again, and once more stooped low.

"I'm going to tackle him," whispered Frank.

Stealthily he advanced until he was only a few yards away from the mysterious stranger. A quick rush and Frank had collared the fellow before he could stir from his tracks. There was a brief struggle.

"You let me be!" gasped the prisoner. "Let me alone. I ain't doing anything."

Frank bundled him back into the alley. Joe, who had heard the sounds of the struggle and thought something had gone wrong, hurried up to them. The captive struggled in vain.

"Let me go!" he demanded. "I ain't doing you any harm."

His voice was familiar. Frank swung him around and they peered at him in the dim light.

"Sidney Pebbles!" gasped Joe.

It was indeed the Sidney Pebbles whom they had met on the dock, the Sidney Pebbles who had vanished so mysteriously from their home on the night of Aunt Gertrude's arrival.

"Well," said Frank, holding the prisoner firmly. "This is a surprise. We've been looking for you, Pebbles. We've been wanting to have a talk with you ever since you left our house."

"My name isn't Pebbles. You've the wrong man," muttered the captive.

"The real Sidney Pebbles works at Lakeside," Joe told him. "You'd better talk or it will be the worse for you. What's your real name?"

"Henry Pinkerton," he muttered sullenly.

"What made you call yourself Sidney Pebbles, then?" demanded Frank.

"Because I look like him. You fellows had better let me go. You may not know it but I'm one of the best detectives in the United States. It'll be just too bad for you if the authorities find out that you've been handling Henry Pinkerton this way."

"So! You're a great detective, are you?" said Frank, who sensed that the fellow was only a pretentious braggart. "What agency do you work for?"

"Well—I don't work for anybody just yet," confessed Pinkerton. "The government and the agencies won't give a fellow a chance. They don't know how good I am. I took a correspondence course in how to be a great detective and I passed with mighty good marks, let me tell you. I'm working on this Chinese case right now and when I solve it I'll be famous."

"What Chinese case?" asked Joe, startled.

"Well, I don't rightly know what it's all about but I was at your father's office one day to see if he would give me a job and I heard him talking to Mr. North. So when he wouldn't give me a job I said to myself that I'd solve that smuggling case, whatever it was, and make a name for myself."

"So that's why you made up an excuse to get into our house?" exclaimed Frank.

"Well, I met your aunt on the boat and I found out where she was going, so I thought it was a good chance to get some inside information. She asked me to get her a drink of water so I put a couple of drops of medicine in it— harmless stuff, wouldn't hurt a fly—just to put her to sleep so she'd go past Bayport."

"Do you realize," said Frank, "that she's been ill ever since?"

"Shucks," said Pinkerton, "I didn't give her enough to hurt anybody."

"Why did you steal the papers from Dad's pockets?" snapped Joe.

"Papers?" exclaimed Pinkerton. "I didn't steal any papers. During the night I got afraid you chaps would find me out so I just sneaked away. But I didn't take anything. I'm not a thief. I'm a detective. And a rattling good one, too," he added.

"Didn't you leave footprints under our living room window?" demanded Frank incredulously.

"No. I went out the front door and down the walk."

This threw a new light on the situation. Who, then, had made those footprints?

"Well, then," said Joe, "didn't you spy on Louie Fong and Orrin North out at North's garage last night?"

"Who is Louie Fong?" replied Pinkerton blankly. "I wasn't anywhere near Mr. North's garage."

"Weren't you prowling around this store today?" asked Frank.

"Nope," said Pinkerton. "I've never been around here before. Just thought I'd investigate the place tonight because I got a tip that someone had seen a Chinaman coming out of the place."

The boys were perplexed. By his stupid interference he had complicated the case from the beginning. They saw, then, that there was an unknown factor in the affair. Someone else had dropped the note and left the footprints beneath the window. Someone else had spied on Louie Fong and Orrin North at the garage. Someone else had been prowling about the secret meeting place in the store that day.

"You've gone and spoiled all my work," growled Pinkerton, "just when I was getting along fine. I don't see why you have to come butting in.''

At that moment there was a warning cry from Tom Wat. Taking no part in the conversation, he had noticed the appearance of several suspicious looking shadows in the gloom of the lane. Back of Louie Fong's laundry he thought he had seen a flash of light. Later he thought he heard a stealthy footstep. He had wanted to be certain before he informed the others. Then he had seen a man run swiftly into the lane from the rear of the store.

At that moment Tom Wat had given the alarm, but he was too late. Half a dozen figures seemed to rise out of the very ground. Frank and Joe sprang around to find themselves confronting three men who bore swiftly down upon them. Henry Pinkerton uttered a howl of fear and took to his heels. He blundered into a man who made a swing at him but missed. Tom Wat had gone scarcely three paces before a man plunged out of the darkness and brought him to the ground.

''We're trapped, Joe!'' gasped Frank, as he tried to fight off the attackers.

The boys battled bravely but they were outnumbered and seized. Struggling, they were hustled out of the alley, but they could not cry out because their captors had roughly gagged them. They were rushed quickly through a doorway at the back of Louie Fong's laundry.

There was a dim light in the shop and its glow revealed the vicious faces of their captors. They had fallen into the hands of half-a-dozen Chinamen.

They were filled with dismay as they were pushed through the back room of the laundry. One of the men knelt and drew open a trap-door. It was not the trap-door through which Frank had previously tumbled. A flight of steps led to the regions beneath.

Still struggling vainly they were hustled down into an underground chamber. A door was flung open, revealing a gloomy, dismal room beyond. Roughly, the boys were thrust inside, and the door was shut with a clang. A key grated in the lock.

They were prisoners underground. Prisoners of Louie Fong. And they knew, now that they were in the power of the merciless China-man, that they might never see the light of day again. Truly, as Sam Lee had said, Louie Fong was always dangerous.

Frank picked himself up from the ground and rubbed his bruises.

"Beaten!" he muttered. "Just when we thought everything was coming along our way."

Tom Wat, although his face was pale, said nothing.

Joe made a grimace of disgust.

"We stepped into a neat trap," he said. "And of course Henry Pinkerton *would* be the only one lucky enough to get away."

Suddenly a harsh voice broke in:

"You catchee Louie Fong, eh? Velly foolish."

There was a burst of maniacal laughter. The boys looked up. There, beyond a tiny grating in the wall, they saw the sinister yellow face of Louie Fong. His teeth were bared in a hideous grin as he gloated over their plight.

"Mellican boy dless up like Chinaboy," he said scornfully. "Mellican boy talkee Mellican talk in alley." He laughed derisively.

Frank flushed as he realized how they had been caught. Someone had been watching them as they came down the alley. Doubtless their disguises had not been penetrated at first, but when they had captured Henry Pinkerton the ruse had been discovered. Frank had forgotten that he was supposed to be a Chinaman. He had spoken in his natural tone of voice. Louie Fong's henchmen, then, had lost no time in surrounding the group and taking them prisoners.

"You might as well let us out of here, Louie Fong," Frank said, trying to show a bold front. "You won't gain anything by it."

Louie Fong cackled with laughter.

"Mebbe Fenton Ha'dy come let you out?"

"Maybe Fenton Hardy won't make it hot for you if anything happens to us," said Joe.

The Chinaman sneered.

"Two, three minute now," he said, "Fenton Ha'dy in samee fix like you."

"What do you mean?" demanded Frank, startled. "He isn't in Bayport."

"You wait," said Louie Fong. An iron shutter swiftly crashed over the grating. The Chinaman's face disappeared.

"What does he mean?" said Joe.

"He means," replied Frank dully, "that Dad is in Bayport. And coming here. The moment he enters the place he will be trapped."

"And we can't do a thing to warn him," groaned Joe.

A moment later the shutter was raised again. Once more they saw the face of Louie Fong, his features twisted in a diabolical smile.

"Mebbe you look-see now," he said.

They rushed to the grating as Louie Fong withdrew. Through the bars the horrified boys gazed on a strange scene.

In a low, smoky room they saw their father, Fenton Hardy. His arms were raised. On a table in front of him sat Orrin North, a revolver in his hand.

# CHAPTER XXV

## THE FOOTPRINTS EXPLAINED

"WELL, Hardy!" the ship owner was saying. "You walked right into the trap, didn't you?"

"So it seems," agreed the detective, with apparent chagrin.

"I was too smart for you that time," Orrin North laughed shortly. "As if I didn't know you were following me today! Why, the minute I got wise I said to myself, 'Follow me, eh? I'll let him follow me right into a trap.' And here you are."

"What do you intend to do about it?" inquired Fenton Hardy.

"I'm going to ask you some questions. That's what I'm going to do first of all. Who set you to followin' me?"

"That's for you to find out."

"I'll tell you what I think," growled North. "I think you're workin' for the authorities. For the government. What I thought you were doing for me, you were doing for my enemy."

"I never accepted your proposition," Fenton Hardy reminded him. "You asked me to work for you in helping to break up the smuggling ring but I never gave you my answer. I didn't trust you, North. I thought I knew why you wanted to engage me. It was to remove suspicion from yourself."

"So you decided to work for the authorities?"

"Exactly."

"And what has it got you?"

"Well," said the detective, "I think I have some evidence against you and Louie Fong. Not as much as I should like to have, but enough to break up your smuggling ring."

"And you're going to use that evidence?"

"If I get out of here—yes."

"Well, you're not going to get out of here long enough to use it. I'll show you what your meddling has brought you. Come here."

He rose from his chair, and still keeping the revolver trained on Fenton Hardy, strode to the door of the chamber in which the boys were imprisoned. He unlocked it and flung the door open. Louie Fong, who emerged from the shadows behind Fenton Hardy, viewed the scene, grinning with delight.

"Look there!" said North.

Fenton Hardy was staggered.

"My boys!" he exclaimed. "How did they get here?"

"By meddlin'. Same as you," Orrin North

told him. He slammed the door before father and sons could exchange a word.

"Now," continued the ship owner, after giving the key a careless twist, "maybe you'll think twice before you turn your evidence over to the authorities."

"You won't harm my sons?" demanded Fenton Hardy incredulously.

There was a shrill, diabolical laugh from Louie Fong.

"Won't we?" said North. "If you turn that evidence over to the authorities you'll never see your boys alive again."

"In that case," said Fenton Hardy, "I must admit defeat."

"But that isn't all," said North. "I don't trust you, Hardy. I don't trust you a bit. You're too slippery. I'm going to get rid of you."

"How?"

"One of my boats is leavin' Bayport tonight, on a voyage to South America. You're goin' to be on that vessel."

The boys felt a thrill of horror as they listened intently to the conversation beyond their prison.

"How can I be sure that my sons will be safe?" asked Fenton Hardy.

"You'll have to trust Louie Fong for that," said North with a wicked, cruel wink toward the Chinaman. "You may as well make up your mind to it, Hardy," the ship owner rasped. "You're through. We're goin' to ship you out of here tonight and you're never comin' back. As for those precious boys of yours, we'll attend to them ourselves. You got yourself into this mess and it's no concern of mine what happens to you as long as you're out of my way. Understand?"

Frank had not been wasting his time. The moment Orrin North had closed the door, he had sprung toward the lock. On the floor of the chamber he had found a small wedge of wood, which he had swiftly slipped into the catch before the ship owner could turn the key.

Frank, now at the door, quietly tested the knob. Had his scheme worked? If it had failed he knew that all hope was lost.

He turned the handle, pulled slightly on the door. It moved. The device had not caught. On this point Frank Hardy had outwitted the sinister jailers.

"You and your boys are better out of the way, so far as me and Louie Fong is concerned," he could hear North snarling. "I'm not takin' any chances on a term in the penitentiary."

Tom Wat sped across the cell and grabbed Frank by the arm. He sensed what the boy had in mind.

"Me run velly klick!" he whispered. "Go get help."

Frank hesitated not a moment. He decided to let Tom Wat make the first attempt to flee. Even if the Chinaman were caught he would occupy the attention of North and Louie Fong sufficiently to open the way to escape on the part of himself and Joe.

He opened the door slightly. Tom Wat peered out, and gestured to Frank as a signal that he was ready. Frank flung the door open, and like a flash his disguised Chinese friend leaped over the threshold. He was halfway across the room before Orrin North or his companion saw him.

There was a screech of rage from Louie Fong, who immediately sprang at the flying figure, but he was too slow. Tom Wat was across the room, had wrenched open the door, and disappeared.

Roaring with fury, Orrin North jumped to his feet. The revolver wavered. In that instant Fenton Hardy, who had been coolly awaiting his opportunity, leaped at him.

At the same moment Frank and Joe sped out of the cell. They were met by Louie Fong, who snatched up a hatchet from the floor, and sent it whizzing through the air. Frank dodged the missile and then crashed against the Chinaman.

The Oriental screeched for help. A door

opened, and three of his servants rushed in from an adjoining room. Confusion prevailed. One could scarcely distinguish friend from foe. Fong was trying desperately to regain possession of his hatchet—he would stop at nothing.

Fenton Hardy and North struggled desperately in the middle of the room. Joe tackled one of the Chinamen and sent him crashing against the wall with a well-aimed blow that caught the fellow on the point of the jaw. Louie Fong, his long fingers grappling at Frank's throat, gasped as the boy's fists smashed against his evil face. He stumbled back. Frank flew at him and they went crashing over the table and plunged to the floor in a flurry of kicking legs and flailing fists. Shouts, groans, shrieks and yells mingled with the thud of blows, the crash of furniture.

Suddenly from outside came a great pounding and clattering, ending in a terrific smash. There was a shot, a thudding of feet on the stairs, a roar of voices. A door swung open. Policemen swarmed into the room.

They swung their clubs right and left. The battle ceased as suddenly as it began. When it was over, Orrin North, Louie Fong and the Chinamen were in handcuffs, aghast and subdued.

"We didn't get any signal, Sir, from you," said a burly officer as he saluted Fenton Hardy, "but when a girl with slanty eyes came up and said there was a murder going on here, we came on a run!"

"Quite right, Officer," replied Fenton Hardy, smiling. "You came in the nick of time. I wasn't in any position to give you a signal as I had promised."

He turned to his sons. "Boys, it was you who saved the day." The fond parent gripped a hand of each of his brave lads.

"But what's the meaning of it, Dad?" demanded Frank when the first joyous greetings were over. "We thought you were out of town, and we knew there was danger here, so we were trying to help solve the mystery."

"I knew there was real danger," he told them. "I realized North was trying to set a trap for me—I have been watching the crook. I had planned to send for help, but of course in the final scrimmage which was so unexpected, I couldn't do that because North had me covered. But the escape, through your efforts, of that girl friend—by the way, who is she? How did you come to be imprisoned here? I want to know all about it."

The story was soon told. Frank and Joe related to their father how they had first become involved in the affair, beginning with the arrival of Henry Pinkerton and the discovery of the footprints under the window. When they explained what they had learned about the activities of the smuggling ring, Fenton Hardy was delighted.

"Just the evidence I need to complete my case!" he exclaimed. "With your friend Sam Lee as a witness I can break up that smuggling ring so thoroughly that it can never be revived."

Once more the Hardy boys had proved their worth; so much so that their father was to send them soon to solve "The Mark on the Door." Just now he was high in his praise.

"I wanted to work secretly on the case," he explained, "and it suited my purpose to have Orrin North believe I had gone away. I never accepted his proposition at any time. As a matter of fact, I went back to the house one night and took the papers in the case from my coat pocket and mailed them to him. I slipped in quietly because I didn't want you to know I was still in Bayport. But I didn't see this impostor of yours—Henry Pinkerton. I looked in the window first, because I wanted to see if everything was all right at home."

"And you lost a note?" exclaimed Joe.

"Did you find it?" said Fenton Hardy. "Yes, I lost a note I had picked up in one of the Chinese places when I was shadowing Louie Fong."

"Then," said Frank solemnly, "Aunt Gertrude *must* have dreamed about that Chinaman after all. And now, I know whose footprints we have been tabulating.''

''Do you?'' said Joe. ''I, too, have a hunch.''

And have you guessed by this time, my readers, that the footprints under the window were those of the famous detective, Fenton Hardy?

**THE END**